## THE ALTERNATIVE IS MURDER

Diego was gazing at him, speechless.

Fox met his gaze and said calmly, "There are eight of you, and one of you is a murderer. And damn dangerous. And damn cunning. And a person of imagination. I doubt if it's you, but if it is, I'm after you and I'll get you. Where did you get that vase? Who is it that wants to kill you? We'll start with the simplest one. Where did you get the vase?"

Diego blurted harshly, "No one wants to kill me!"

"Then take the alternative. Why did you try to kill me?"

**REX STOUT**
**THE BROKEN VASE**

AND BE A VILLAIN
AND FOUR TO GO
THE BROKEN VASE
CHAMPAGNE FOR ONE
CURTAINS FOR THREE
DEATH OF A DUDE
A FAMILY AFFAIR
THE FATHER HUNT
FER-DE-LANCE
THE FINAL DEDUCTION
GAMBIT
MURDER BY THE BOOK
PLOT IT YOURSELF
PRISONER'S BASE
THE RED BOX
THE RUBBER BAND
SECOND CONFESSION
SOME BURIED CAESAR
THREE DOORS TO DEATH
THREE FOR THE CHAIR
THREE MEN OUT
THREE WITNESSES
TOO MANY CLIENTS
TOO MANY WOMEN

# THE BROKEN VASE

## Rex Stout

BANTAM BOOKS
TORONTO • NEW YORK • LONDON • SYDNEY • AUCKLAND

THE BROKEN VASE

*A Bantam Book / published by arrangement with the
Estate of the Author*

*PRINTING HISTORY*
*Farrar & Rinehart edition published 1941*
*Bantam edition / April 1982*
*2nd printing . . . . . April 1983*
*3rd printing . . . . . May 1986*

ISBN 0-553-25632-7

*Published simultaneously in the United States and Canada*

*Bantam Books are published by Bantam Books, Inc. Its trade-
mark, consisting of the words "Bantam Books" and the por-
trayal of a rooster, is Registered in U.S. Patent and Trademark
Office and in other countries. Marca Registrada. Bantam
Books, Inc., 666 Fifth Avenue, New York, New York 10103.*

PRINTED IN THE UNITED STATES OF AMERICA

H    11 10 9 8 7 6 5 4 3

# THE BROKEN VASE

# 1

ON THAT raw March night chilling drafts swirled treacherously around the corners backstage at Carnegie Hall—the icy puffs and currents which on bygone nights had sent a perspiring Paderewski or Heifetz or Chaliapin in headlong flight to the dressing room and had kept Melba's or Sembrich's maid vigilantly on guard at the door to the stage, with an ermine wrap ready for the diva's hot bare damp shoulders. That, of course, was at the intermission or the end; it was now only eight-fifteen and nothing had happened yet on the great bare stage to make a strong man perspire. Any one who thinks a violin virtuoso is not a strong man should try the "Devil's Trill" with muscles of anything less than steel.

It must be admitted, however, that Jan Tusar, who in a quarter of an hour was supposed to walk on the stage with nothing but a fiddle and a bow and prove his right to stand where Ysaye and Kreisler had stood, did not at that moment look strong. He had just emerged from the dressing room and stood there on the threshold, with one hand gripping the rim of the door and the other the neck of his violin just above the pegs. Though he was six feet tall, he looked like a frightened boy, with his set face and widened eyes, and his lower lip pulled in by his teeth. Of a dozen or more people scattered around, all were looking at him except a man in fireman's uniform standing unobtrusively by a far wall, who had doubtless learned that an artist, during that terrible last half hour, is as unpredictable as a racehorse at the barrier, and nothing can be done about it. Among the others, at their various locations and distances, there was a general movement as if they would approach, but it was immediately restrained

1

except in the case of a woman, not young, who with long bony fingers was keeping a sable wrap closed at her throat.

But a man moved swiftly to intercept her, and she gave it up with a shrug after an acid glance at the broad back which had interposed itself between her and the frightened boy.

Jan Tusar's wide eyes moved to focus on the man's face, but he said nothing.

The man put a white pudgy hand on the violinist's shoulder. "You go back in there and sit down," he said persuasively. His voice was a deep rumble with a rasp of asperity, in spite of his obvious desire to be sympathetic and reassuring. He was Tusar's height, but much heavier and more than twice as old, something over fifty—well-fed, well-groomed in his evening elegance, palpably well-placed in whatever orbit he inhabited. His hand was light but firm on the youth's shoulder. "This won't do, Jan. Sit down and take it easy until you're called...."

"My hands are cold," Tusar complained. There was scarcely controlled terror in his voice. "They won't get warm. My fingers are stiff—What time is it?"

"A quarter past eight. You must—"

"Where's Mrs. Pomfret?"

"She went home. She made Henry take her home. You shouldn't have—"

"Let me alone! I'm all right. But I wish she—who's that over there with Diego?"

"Diego Zorilla?" The man turned to look. "I don't know."

"His eyes looked right through me! What's that sticking out of his pocket?" Tusar's voice was petulant and aggrieved. "Coming to a concert with his pockets stuffed full of packages! Diego! Come here, will you?"

Diego came trotting—a stocky man somewhat older than Tusar, not as tall, with swarthy skin and black eyes and hair.

"Well, Jan!" he exclaimed cheerfully. "May Orpheus ride your bow!"

"Thanks, Diego. Who's that with you? I want to meet him."

"Why, he's a friend...we didn't..."

"I want to meet him."

"Very well, of course." Diego turned to beckon with his finger, and the other man crossed to join them. Of medium size and height, in his early thirties, there was nothing remarkable about his appearance unless you met directly the swift penetration of his brown eyes or were observant enough to note the smooth and effortless power of his movement. Before he had stopped beside Diego Zorilla, Tusar demanded:

"Why did you look at me like that? What have you got in your pocket?"

"This is my friend," Diego said sharply. "Naturally, Jan, you are in a state, but you are not a child. My friend's name is Mr. Tecumseh Fox, Mr. Jan Tusar." He included the elegant older man, still there: "Mr. Adolph Koch." His voice sharpened again: "You have heard me speak of Mr. Fox. He is one who at my request contributed to the purchase—"

"Please!" Fox cut him off, hastily and peremptorily.

"Oh," Tusar said with a frown of irritation, glancing at the violin in his hand as if he had forgotten it was there. "This—you helped—" Suddenly his face and voice changed completely; he was charmingly ashamed and contrite. "I'm sorry—I'm damn sorry—"

"Forget it," said Fox bluntly, smiling at him. "Diego shouldn't have mentioned it, and he shouldn't have dragged me back here anyway. My manners are defective. I have a habit of staring at people. I apologize. This—" he slapped the package protruding from his side pocket—"is a carton of cigarettes. Another bad habit."

"A carton?" The youth tittered. "A whole carton?" He started to laugh, but it was more like a squeak, nervous and high-pitched. "You hear that, Mr. Koch? A whole carton in his pocket! That's the funniest—that's worse even than you—" His shrill laughter, crescendo and accelerando, pierced the air.

There was a general stir and movement, and shocked ejaculations. A man, apparently buried in gloom and foreboding, who had been standing ten paces off, ran up and grabbed Adolph Koch by the elbow, muttering at him. Others approached, the woman in sable with a determined stride jostling Tecumseh Fox, who promptly retreated to his former position near the passage to the stage and surveyed the scene from there. In a moment he was joined by his friend Zorilla, who was shaking his head darkly and mumbling to himself.

Fox spoke to Zorilla's ear, not to shout against the confused half-hysterical babel: "Do you tell me this is a conventional prelude to a violin recital?"

"There is nothing conventional," the other growled savagely, "about what is happening here. I know. I tried it once." He held up his left hand. On it the middle and third fingers were only pitiful stubs, chopped off below the knuckle. "Before that happened."

"Yes, but—"

"But nothing. In two hours Jan will be established on the peak or he will have tumbled into a crevasse, perhaps never to climb out again."

"I understand that, but who the devil are those others? Why doesn't someone—who is that clawing at the skeleton in sable?"

"That's Felix Beck, Jan's teacher and coach."

"Who's the pretty girl hugging herself and looking scared to death?"

"Dora Mowbray, Jan's accompanist. Naturally she is scared. Her father was my manager, and also Jan's—you know, Lawton Mowbray, who fell from his office window a few months ago and smashed on the pavement. The tall young chap pushing the others away is Perry Dunham, the son of Mrs. Pomfret. Irene Dunham Pomfret—you know about her. Her son by her first husband."

"Where is she?"

Diego shrugged. "I don't know. Perhaps out front in her box. I would have expected her to be here."

"Who—for God's sake, coming out of the dressing room! They were in there too! Who is it?"

"You know her."

"No, I don't."

"Look again. You go to movies."

"Not often. Is she one of them?"

"Yes, indeed. It's Hebe Heath. I don't know who that young fellow is with her. Look at her pulling at Jan, and look at Koch watching her."

"I don't want to." Fox sounded disgusted. "Some one with a little sense ought to wade into that. Let's go out to our seats."

Diego nodded. "It's nearly time. Only a minute or two." His black eyes were aimed across at Jan Tusar, still at the dressing-room door, surrounded by confusion and clamor. "It's a terrible thing for a boy, that long walk onto that stage, with your fingers hot and moist on the strings—or cold and dry is even worse. Come on, Fox, this way."

At their seats, on the aisle in the tenth row, orchestra, of the vast auditorium, Diego, after disposing of his hat and coat, stood for a moment to survey the house. It was crowded, with the few remaining seats being rapidly filled by last-minute arrivals, but that, as he well knew, was without significance; any competent manager undertaking a Carnegie Hall debut would know how to provide for that. Besides, there was Mrs. Pomfret, not to mention lesser luminaries busily brightening the path of young artists to fame and fortune. Diego, noting faces here and there, especially in the boxes above, saw that they had done a good job for Jan Tusar.

Or, rather, there had been, not there was, Mrs. Pomfret, for she was not to be seen. Sitting down, Diego murmured to Fox's ear, "Mystery. Case for you. No Mrs. Pomfret. She always has Box FF, and it's empty."

Fox nodded absently and continued to look at his program. Dora Mowbray at the piano. "Introduction and Rondo Capriccioso, Op. 28, Saint-Saens." "Pastorale and Scherzo, Op. 8, Lalo." That meant nothing to him. He turned a page. Program notes by Philip Turner. His habit of buying things at odd moments and stuffing them in his pockets might really be better controlled; on the other hand, if he felt like taking a carton of Dixies home to Crocker who would smoke no other brand, why shouldn't he? He glanced at his watch; it was eight-forty. *It was one of Sarasate's favorite program numbers, and he played it with a sprightliness and charm....*

The lights dimmed, a rustle of expectation rippled over the audience and subsided, the door at the left of the stage opened, and a young woman in an apricot-colored gown appeared and walked across to the piano. There were a few scattered handclaps, to which she paid no attention. Her face was so pale that it was no better than a vague blur above the apricot dress, and Fox thought it was ridiculous that no one had had gumption enough to put some make-up on her. He was admiring the neat unity of her brow and nose and chin in profile as she sat motionless on the bench, her head bowed, when the door opened again and a burst of applause greeted the hero of the evening. Jan Tusar walked with stiff but not ungraceful strides to the middle of all that space and a little beyond, bowed to the greeting with no smile, bowed again, waited a moment, and, before the hands had become completely quiet, turned his head for a glance at Dora Mowbray. Her hands moved, a tinkle came, and Tusar raised his violin and tucked its heel into its nest under his chin.

From the corner of his eye Fox saw Diego's left hand, the one with two fingers gone, taking a convulsive grip on his right wrist, just as Tusar's bow danced into the opening which, according to the program notes, was "an adorable andante malinconico."

Nothing happened. That is, nothing exploded. The audience listened politely and quietly, there was only the normal amount of coughing and program rustling, and melodious and harmonious sounds came from the violin and piano. To Tecumseh Fox, who never went to concerts, it seemed not at all unpleasant and even mildly enjoyable; but toward the end he became aware of a feeling of uneasiness. Surely Diego's breathless unrelenting rigidity was carrying good behavior to an extreme; and what was the little man on the right shaking his head about?

But when the sound from the stage stopped and Tusar

stood there erect with his face white and grim and drawn, and the sound from the audience's hands was manifestly a perfunctory and embarrassed necessity empty of enthusiasm, Fox leaned over to demand of his companion's ear, "What's the matter? Did he play the wrong piece?"

Diego shook his head and said nothing, but Fox heard the woman in front of him whispering to her escort, "I don't understand it. I never heard so dead a tone, and I've heard plenty. If he goes on like that it's a crime not to stop him...."

On the stage Tusar nodded at Dora Mowbray, and the second number began. It sounded to Fox much as it had before, only, after a few minutes, it seemed to him that there was a distinct increase in audible little noises from the audience. He began to feel uncomfortable, and his legs were crossed wrong and had to be changed. The little man at his right was openly fidgeting and let his program fall to the floor. At the end of the Lalo piece the applause was even more perfunctory than before. Fox forwent any glance at Diego; he merely changed legs again, and prayed that the remaining number before the intermission—according to the program, "Obertass" by Wieniawski—would be short. It was. So was the acclaim from the audience, but Tusar's acknowledgment of it was even shorter. His face set and pale, he stood and stared straight front for one second, then pivoted on his heel and marched off. The audience buzzed and hummed and fluttered. Dora Mowbray, her face even whiter than Tusar's had been, waited a moment on the piano bench, then jumped up and ran across to the door and was gone.

"Come on, growled Diego, stooping for his hat and coat, and Fox got his own and followed up the aisle. In the lobby Diego growled again, "I've got to have a drink," and, when Fox nodded agreement, led the way outside and down the sidewalk to a bar.

Fox sipped a highball and watched the Spaniard down two double Scotches in succession, judging from the expression on the other's face that conversation was not in order. For that matter, he was himself somewhat embarrassed and would not have known what to say. A year ago he had, at Diego's solicitation, contributed two thousand dollars toward the purchase of a violin for a young virtuoso who, according to Diego, was or would be another Sarasate; and he had been brought here this evening to witness a triumph in which he might feel that he had a trifling share. So now he was not only embarrassed; he was somewhat irritated. He hadn't wanted to come. He knew nothing about music. He had not invited the feeling that he had bought a right to share in another man's triumph. He continued to sip his highball in silence, while his companion frowned gloomily at the row of bottles back of the bar.

Suddenly Diego turned his head. "You don't know what happened in there. Do you?"

Fox put his empty glass down and said, "No."

"Neither do I."

"I suppose," said Fox, trying not to sound annoyed, "he was so scared he couldn't pull himself together. He certainly looked like it."

Diego shook his head. "No, it wasn't that. His fingering was all right, even his portamento. I don't understand it. It was the tone. Dead. Absolutely dead! That fiddle should sing! And he was fighting—his courage was incredible, he fought right up to the end! But did you hear it? It might have been a piece of junk from a pawnshop. I don't understand it. I feel a little the way I did when this happened." He displayed the hand with two fingers. "If you'll excuse me, I'll walk a while and maybe drink a little. I don't think I feel like talking."

"What about Tusar?" Fox demanded.

"I don't know."

"Will he try to finish?"

"I don't know. I tell you I don't understand it."

"Neither do I, but I'd like to. I thought it was funk, but you say it wasn't. Let's go back and see him. And his violin."

"It won't do any good. It's all over for this time. Half of the audience has gone home. Anyway, he can't fight any harder than he did." Diego shuddered. "I wouldn't go through that again for a finger."

But Fox insisted, and urged the necessity for haste if they were to get backstage before the end of the intermission. He paid for the drinks and hurried out, with the other still reluctant beside him. As they passed the front of the hall on their way to the corner, people were straggling down the steep steps from the entrance, hatted and wrapped, obviously with no intention of returning.

There was no one to challenge them at the stage door, which would have been remarkable if they had been in a mood to remark on such an irregularity. They climbed steps, passed along a corridor, turned a couple of corners, crossed a large room cluttered with everything from bunting to sawhorses, and opened a door.

There had been a dozen people there before; now there were twice as many. And if before the atmosphere had been one of tense and nervous expectation, it was now, to Fox's swift encompassing glance, one of shocked incredulous horror. The only faces that did not share it were those of two policemen in uniform who stood with their backs to the wall, one on each side of the door to the dressing room, which was closed. Nearest to Fox and Diego was Adolph Koch, seated on the edge of a wooden chair, as elegant as ever except that he was breathing with his mouth open. Diego confronted him and demanded:

"What is it?"

"What?" Koch lifted his head. "Oh. Jan. Committed suicide. Shot himself."

## 2

ONE OF the policemen tramped over and inquired, "How did you fellows get in here? Isn't there a man out there?"

Diego turned to look at him, but couldn't speak.

"It's all right," Fox told him. "We came by the stage door. We belong."

"Belong to what?"

"They're friends of Mr. Tusar's," said Koch, and the policeman nodded and let it go.

Diego stood staring at the dressing-room door, his face contorted like a man trying to lift something too heavy for him.

Fox sidled to a corner and surveyed the scene. He did that both from instinct and from habit. He had at one time regarded that diathesis as a defect of his organism, and still was not fond of it, but an extended and sometimes painful experience had forced him to accept the fact. Events and situations which caused the blood of most people to rush in hot torrents, or froze it in their veins, merely turned him into an instrument of precision for record and appraisal. Whether he liked it or not, that was perforce his function in the face of tragedy, while others might lament or console or collapse.

Of those visible, none had collapsed. They were here and there in pairs and groups, gazing silently at the door of the dressing room or murmuring in hushed tones. A woman was trying not to giggle, and a man and another woman were gripping her arm and telling her to stop. Felix Beck, Jan Tusar's teacher, was pacing up and down, washing his hands in air. Diego Zorilla, having found speech, was talking with Adolph Koch. Hebe Heath was not to be seen, but the young man who had been in the dressing room with her previously, whom Diego had not known, was standing across the room with his hands in his pockets, and Fox noted that he also seemed to fancy himself as a recording and appraising instrument. Then Fox frowned, moved involuntarily, and stopped again, as his gaze was directed at Dora Mowbray. She was on a chair by the opposite wall, and on her face, no longer white but a sickly gray, there was no expression whatever or sign that she was hearing the words being addressed to her by Perry Dunham, who was leaning over her and talking earnestly to her ear.

Everyone turned as the door opened and three men

entered. They were not in uniform, but the manner of their entry proclaimed them. One of the policemen called, "In here, Captain," and the man in front, after a rapid glance around, crossed the room briskly and then stopped and turned. His air and attitude were businesslike but not aggressive, and when he spoke his voice, not raised, was affable almost to the point of apology.

"If you please," he said, "it will save time if you'll give your names and addresses to these men. Please don't fuss about it now."

He turned again and opened the door of the dressing room, and after one of the policemen followed him in the door was closed. The other two men got out notebooks and pencils and started on their task. The arrival of competent authority seemed to have absorbed some of the general shock and tension; people moved, and murmurs became audible words. Fox stuck to his corner. There, in due course, he was approached by a man with a notebook.

"Name, please?"

"Tecumseh Fox."

"How do you spell?..."

Fox spelled it, and repeated it, "Tecumseh Fox, Brewster, New York."

"Occupation, please?"

"Private detective."

"Huh?" The man looked up. "Oh, sure. You're that one." He finished writing. "You here on business?"

"Nope. My night off."

The man grunted, made the astonishing statement, "You look more like a chess player," in a tone of detachment, and moved on.

Fox unobtrusively made his way to the other side of the room, to the neighborhood of the young man Diego didn't know, and got close enough to learn that his name was Theodore Gill and that he practiced the calling of publicity agent. When the census taker had passed on, the young man suddenly turned, met Fox's eyes with an amused grin, and inquired:

"Did you get it all right? Theodore Gill. My friends call me Ted."

Fox, a little taken aback, paid the grin with a smile. He noted that the eyes were more gray than blue, and the hair more light-brown than yellow, as he explained, "I thought I knew you, but I guess I don't. My name's Fox."

The other nodded. "Sure, I know. I know everything and everybody because I have to, God help me. Which do you think is worse—ah, here comes the science squad. They even beat the medical—no, here he is too. Look at that, would you? We are the universal necessity of the modern world. I mean publicity agents, of which I am one. Without us no one can live, and some poor devils can't even die. They'll take a hundred pictures of him. By the way, didn't I hear you say you came in by the stage door?"

"I expect so. I said it."

"Did you happen to see an entrancing vision of breathtaking beauty anywhere around? Momentarily blond?"

"If you mean Hebe Heath, no. Have you lost her?"

"I hope not. She was here, but isn't."

"Are you her—uh—"

"I'm her trumpet-tongued herald. She's a client of mine. If ever you need—but that can wait, and must. Here's the third act."

The captain had emerged from the dressing room and pulled the door to behind him. His hat and overcoat had been discarded. The deliberate sweep of his eyes took them all in, and his manner was a shade more aggressive than it had been, but his voice was grave and informative rather than hostile or meancing:

"Mr. Jan Tusar is dead from a bullet that entered his open mouth and came out at the top of his skull. The official conclusion at present is that he shot himself, and there is no reason to suppose that it will be changed. He left a brief note—" the captain raised his hand to display a slip of paper—"addressed 'To my friends who believed in me.' I won't read it now. The handwriting will be authenticated by experts, but I would like to have it tentatively verified now by one of you who is familiar with Tusar's writing. Will someone do that, please?"

There were glances, movements, hesitations, murmurs. A voice came out of the subdued confusion:

"I will."

"Thank you. Your name?"

"Beck. Felix Beck." He stepped forward. His mouth opened without any sound emerging, and then he said loudly as though to establish for all time an important and immortal fact, "I am Tusar's teacher. For years I am his teacher."

"Good." The captain handed him the paper. "Is that his handwriting?"

Beck took it and peered at it, in a complete silence except for muffled voices and sounds of activity that came from behind the closed door of the dressing room. He rubbed the back of his hand across his eyes and looked again, his lips moving as he read the words. Then he looked up at the faces and spoke in a low quaver, "Do you know what he says to us?" He shook the paper at them. "I am one of them, am I not? His friends who believed in him? I ask you! Do you know—" Two tears rolled down his cheeks, and he couldn't go on.

The captain said sharply, "Mr. Beck! I'm asking you. Is this Tusar's writing?" He reached and got the paper.

Beck nodded, swiped at his eyes again, and shouted, "Yes! Of course it is!"

"Thank you." The captain put the paper in his pocket. "Now a few questions, and that will be all. Were any of you in this room at the time Tusar left the stage and came to the dressing room?"

Felix Beck spoke again. "I was."

"You saw him enter the dressing room?"

"Yes." Beck's voice was more controlled. "I was at the listening hole outside, but I came here after the Lalo. I couldn't—I came away. I went in the dressing room and came out again, and was here when he came through."

"What did you go in the dressing room for?"

"I wanted to look at the violin case."

"Why?"

"Because I wanted to see. I did not think it was his

violin he was playing." A stir and murmur sounded, and
Beck looked around defiantly. "I still do not think so!"

The captain was frowning. "Why not?"

"Because the sound! Good God, I can hear, can't I?"

"You mean it didn't sound right? Was Tusar's violin a
specially good one?"

"It is a Stradivarius. Not only a Stradivarius, but the
Oksmann. Is that sufficient?"

"I don't know. Didn't Tusar have it with him when he
came here from the stage?"

"Of course he did. But he wouldn't stop. I spoke to him,
but he didn't answer. He walked on by, not looking at me,
and entered the dressing room and shut the door. I went
and started to open it and spoke to him, but he called to
me to keep out. I thought I would let him alone for a
little, and then Miss Mowbray came, and Mr. Koch, and
Mr. Dunham, and then others—"

"When you went in the dressing room to look at the
violin case, was there anyone in there?"

Beck stared. "Anyone— Of course not!"

"Did you see a gun in the dressing room?"

"I didn't see one, no. But it was in his overcoat—at
least it always was. Since he played at a benefit for
Czechoslovakia, and got threatening letters, he has always
carried one. I told him it was foolish, but he did it."

"I see." The captain nodded. "So it was his own gun.
You say Miss Mowbray was the first one to appear after
Tusar. Who is she?"

"She is Tusar's accompanist—"

"This is Miss Mowbray," a voice snapped, "and it's
about time she was taken out of here. She's in no condition to answer a lot of unnecessary questions."

The young man who spoke—handsome, dark-eyed and
dark-haired, fully as elegant in evening attire as Adolph
Koch, and considerably more slender and athletic—had a
hand on the back of Dora Mowbray's chair. His tone,
while not exactly supercilious, conveyed the impression
that if he had the time and felt like it he might do his
grandmother the favor of teaching her to suck eggs. The

captain's eyes took him in, as did others. The captain inquired:

"Your name, please?"

"My name's Perry Dunham. There's no need to question Miss Mowbray. She's already passed out once. She and I both saw Jan shoot himself."

"Oh. You did?"

"We did, as most of the people present can tell you. When I got back here Miss Mowbray and Mr. Koch were already here, and a lot of others came soon after. Everybody buzzed around, wondering what was wrong with Jan. Two or three of them started to go in the dressing room, but he yelled at them to stay out. Finally, when the intermission time was about up, Beck and Koch decided Miss Mowbray should go in, but I thought he might even throw something at her, so I went along. He was standing in front of the mirror with the pistol in his hand. I kept my head and told Miss Mowbray to shut the door and she did. I started talking to Jan, and getting closer to him, but when I was still ten feet away he stuck the gun in his mouth and pulled the trigger."

"Well." The captain took a breath. "As I said, Mr. Dunham, I had already concluded that Tusar committed suicide. I never heard of a man holding his mouth open for someone to stick a gun in it pointing straight up. Of course this settles it, but as a matter of form I'll ask Miss Mowbray a question. Did this thing occur as Mr. Dunham describes it, Miss Mowbray?"

Without looking at him, without lifting her head or eyes to look at anyone, she nodded.

"I'm sorry," the captain persisted, "but if we get it clear now that ends it. You were present, with Mr. Dunham, when Tusar shot himself?"

"Yes." She whispered it. Then her head came up and her eyes met the captain's, and her voice was suddenly and surprisingly strong. "While we stood there—as Perry said. I was farther away than he was, keeping myself—trying not to scream at him. When he lifted the gun Perry jumped for him, but it was—he couldn't—"

"He was too fast," said Dunham curtly. "Or I was too slow. He went down and I stumbled and went down too. When I got up Miss Mowbray had backed up against the door and didn't realize her weight was holding it against someone's effort to open it. I didn't think there ought to be a mob rushing in there, but I didn't know what else to do, so I went and got her away from the door and opened it, and in they came."

The captain grunted. He rubbed his chin, looked slowly around at the faces, and grunted again. "Well," he said, "I don't see any point in bothering you people. We have your names if we need them, but I don't suppose we will. I understand that one of the officers phoned Tusar's sister. Has she come?"

Shaken heads gave him a negative. He went on, "It would be a good idea if a couple of you who are friends of hers would wait here for her. The rest of you might as well go. Unless anyone has something to add to what has been said."

His eyes made the round again. Silence seemed to be all he was to get, until a voice rumbled:

"There's one little thing."

It was Adolph Koch, who had left his chair and was standing in the middle of the room. The captain's eyes settled on him.

"Yes, sir?"

"Where the other note went to."

"The other?..."

"You say Tusar left a note addressed to his friends who believed in him. But soon after the shot was heard several of us entered the dressing room, and though there was a good deal of confusion I heard Mr. Gill say, 'Here's a note he left,' and Miss Mowbry said, 'There are two notes,' and Mr. Gill said, 'No, there's only one,' and Miss Mowbray said, 'There are two, I saw them there together.'" Koch sighed. "I suppose it's of no importance, but in case you think it desirable to search for the other note before we leave..."

The captain was scowling distastefully; this intrusion of a

nasty little complication like a missing note in a perfectly straightforward suicide was most unwelcome. He addressed Dora Mowbray with a tone more aggressive than he had previously used:

"Is that right? Did you say there were two notes?"

She nodded with a heavy head. "I guess I did. I thought I saw two—but of course I was wrong. I saw them when I was standing there and Jan had the gun and Perry was getting closer to him. It was just an impression—it must have been wrong, because Perry says he only saw one. Oh, does it matter?"

The captain bore down. "Then you are not prepared to state positively that you saw two notes?"

"Oh, no—there must have been only one—"

"You saw only one, Mr. Dunham?"

"Of course." The youth darted an unfriendly glance at Adolph Koch. The older man ignored it and said in a skeptical tone to the girl:

"You have very good eyes, Dora." He looked at the captain: "It really does seem probable that there were two notes and that someone took one of them."

The captain demanded testily, "What's your name?"

"Adolph Koch. Manufacturer of dresses and suits. Admirer of the arts."

"Do you make a point of this? Do you think I'm going to ask these ladies and gentlemen to permit me to search their persons?"

"By no means." Koch was unperturbed. "I wouldn't even permit you to search me. I mentioned the matter only because you asked if anyone had anything to add."

"Well, have you anything else?"

"No."

"Has anyone?"

The expression on the captain's face did not invite further contributions, but one came. A baritone inquired politely, "May I make a suggestion?"

Another voice spoke from the rear, "That's Tecumseh Fox, Captain."

"Here as a spectactor only, " Fox got in hastily. "I was

just going to suggest, before you send us off, do you think
it would be a good plan to have Mr. Beck take a look at
that violin? In view of his doubt of its identity?"

"Certainly, I wasn't forgetting that, of course—"

"Before we leave? If you don't mind?"

The captain addressed Felix Beck: "Can you identify
Tusar's violin?"

"Naturally," Beck replied, as though he had been asked
if he could identify his own face in a mirror.

"All of you please remain a moment," said the captain,
and went to the dressing room and entered, closing the
door behind him. There was a cessation of the other
muffled sounds from within; voices could be heard, but
not words; and then the captain reappeared. He closed the
door and turned to confront them, and the scowl on his
face was considerably more pronounced than it had been
when Koch had raised the question of the notes. He
surveyed the audience for a long moment in silence, and
when he spoke his tone was one of dry disgust.

"There's no violin in there."

Ejaculations, gasps, startled movements were the response to that. Felix Beck darted for the dressing-room
door, but one of the census takers grabbed him by the arm
and held him. Half a dozen people were declaring that it
was impossible, they had seen it there, and the captain
was lifting a hand to restore the meeting to order when
the confusion gained a new recruit from without. The door
at the far end burst open and a woman entered—her mink
coat flying open, her dark agitated eyes in her pale face
seeing none of them, her red lips parted for panting. She
rushed across through the lane they made, toward the
dressing room, until she was stopped by the captain, who
blocked her way.

Adolph Koch marched toward her, calling sharply, "Garda!
You shouldn't have—"

She was clawing at the captain. "My brother! Jan!
Where is he—"

Tecumseh Fox quietly retreated to the corner he had
pre-empted before.

# 3

"I DON'T agree," Diego Zorilla said with conviction. "I don't agree at all. It was a sensible thing for Jan to do. I should have done it myself when I lost my fingers. As for the violin, I don't believe it. If any substitution had been made, Jan couldn't possibly have failed to know it." He drank, put the glass down, and shook his head. "No, it was simply stolen, that's all. Though how and by whom…"

"Yes, you might let me in on that," Fox suggested.

They were sitting in Rusterman's Bar, having finally left Carnegie Hall around midnight. The last two hours there had been productive of no result whatever, except the negative one that Jan Tusar's violin could not be found. There seemed to be no question that it had been in the dressing room immediately after Tusar had shot himself. Everyone denied having removed it or even touched it, but it was generally admitted that in the confusion and excitement it could easily have been taken without observation. A careful check had established with a fair amount of certainty that only three people had left the scene before the arrival of the captain: a Mrs. Briscoe, a Mr. Tillingsley, and Miss Hebe Heath. Men had been sent to interview them, and they had all denied any knowledge of the violin. It was true that there had been overcoats and women's wraps around, under one of which the instrument could easily have been carried unseen, and any of those present might have been away for a few minutes without its being remarked, but a search of the entire building was fruitless.

In the comfortable little booth at Rusterman's, Diego had told Fox that of the three persons who had left the scene before the arrival of the police, Mrs. Briscoe was the

19

lady whom Fox had characterized as a skeleton in sable and could be dismissed from consideration as a fiddle thief; Mr. Tillingsley was the concert master of the Manhattan Symphony Orchestra, equally above suspicion; and, though Hebe Heath was a movie star and therefore not subject to the normal processes of reason or logic, it seemed unlikely that she would steal a violin to the purchase of which she had contributed the substantial sum of two thousand, five hundred dollars.

Fox inquired, "Is she also an admirer of the arts?"

"She was an admirer of Jan Tusar," said Diego in a certain tone. "Jan was a very romantic figure. He was, in fact, truly romantic—as he proved tonight. And as I am not. I am a realist. When my fingers were smashed in an accident and they had to go, taking the best of me with them, did I finish the job? Not me. I accepted your hospitality—your charity—and for months stayed at your place in the country, because a realist has to eat. Shall we have another drink? And now I arrange music for the Metropolitan Broadcasting Company."

"A lot of people listen to it. Anyhow, you're all right. Tell me about some of those other people."

Diego told him. It was understood, he said, that Tusar had entertained the idea of marrying Dora Mowbray, but it had not been encouraged by Dora and had been unrelentingly opposed by her father. When, a few months ago, Lawton Mowbray had tumbled from his office window to his death, there had even been murmurs about the possibility that Jan Tusar had sent him on that last journey in order to remove an obstacle from the path of true love; but, Diego said, that had been merely a drop of acid from rumor's unclean tongue, for Jan hadn't been so romantic as all that. After an interval Dora had consented to act again as Jan's accompanist; firstly, because Jan insisted that otherwise he could not play, and secondly, because she needed the money; for, though Lawton Mowbray had been an extremely successful manager of artists, he had spent more than he had made and had left nothing but debts, pleasant memories, and a penniless daughter.

Fox remarked that young Mr. Dunham seemed to be on terms with Miss Mowbray.

Diego snorted and said he hoped not. Perry Dunham was an arrogant young ape, incapable of appreciating one of so true a loveliness as little Dora. He called her "little Dora" because when he had first met her, six years ago, she had been only fourteen and had legs like a calf. Even now, he admitted, she lacked somewhat in roundness for a Spaniard's taste, but she was undeniably lovely, and she could even make pretty good music. As for Perry, he thought swing was music, which—judging from Diego's tone—settled him. The only reason he ever set foot inside Carnegie Hall was to keep on the good side of his rich mother, Irene Dunham Pomfret, who was the financial godmother of enough musicians to make up a Bethlehem Festival. Garda Tusar, Jan's sister, was more his type than Dora Mowbray.

Were they?...

No, not that Diego knew of. The dark and tempestuous Garda, as Fox had himself had opportunity to observe, exhibited in her face and figure and movements the authentic ingredients of a seductress, but if she was using them to that end she was being extremely discreet about it. She was in fact somewhat of a mystery. She was supposed to be working at some vague sort of job connected with the fashion world, but if her salary paid for the clothes she wore and the apartment she maintained and her car and chauffeur, it must be a super-job.

She had been fond of her brother, Fox said.

Undoubtedly, Diego agreed; but recently there had been a coolness. Only yesterday Jan had told him that Garda was so angry with him that she was not coming to the Carnegie Hall recital, but he had not said what she was angry about. Diego added remorsefully that for the past few months he had not maintained his former close relations with Jan, and that had been wrong because it had been his, Diego's, fault; he had been envious. In his remorse, and after six or seven drinks, he admitted it. Jan had been preparing for the most important event of his career; it would assuredly be a glorious triumph; and it was a little more than Diego could bear. He had neglected his young friend at the moment of his greatest need, and he would never forgive himself. Now he would do what he could to atone for it. He would avenge the contemptible treachery that had plunged Jan into a false but fatal despair and caused him to take his life. He would, with his friend Fox's help, discover who it was that had substituted a cracker box with a handle for Jan's violin and had taken it away after it had fulfilled its base purpose. He would ...

Ten minutes later he was saying that if any substitution had been made, Jan couldn't possibly have failed to know it.

Fox smiled at him. "You can't have it both ways, Diego. A little while ago you said—"

"What if I did?" Diego met the smile with sour gloom. "Anyway, I was right. It's all well enough to say Jan couldn't have been fooled about that violin, but he was. And I'm going to find out who did it. I'm drunk now, but I won't be tomorrow, and that's exactly what I'm going to do."

"Well, good luck." Fox looked at his watch. "I'm sorry I can't be here to help, but I'm catching a sleeper to Louisville. Two days should be all I need there, so I'll probably be giving you a ring Thursday morning to ask how you're making out."

But at Louisville a problem regarding a sudden and unaccountable epidemic of stomach-aches in a stable of racehorses, among them a Derby entry, took a day longer than Fox had expected, so it was Friday instead of Thursday when he returned to New York, at two in the afternoon instead of eight in the morning, and at LaGuardia Airport instead of the Pennsylvania Station. He did not, however, need to phone Diego Zorilla to learn how he was making out with his project of atonement and vengeance, because he had talked with him over long distance Thursday evening and already knew. Furthermore, he had received information and a request which now resulted in his eating a hasty lunch in the airport lunchroom, taking a subway to Manhattan, and a taxi to an address on Park Avenue.

His fatigue after three strenuous days and nights, his pockets bulging with packages—gifts for the Trimbles and others at the Zoo, as his home in the country was popularly called—and the battered suitcase he was carrying, should naturally, he thought, have caused some degree of aloofness on the part of the impeccable butler who admitted him to a spacious reception hall after an elevator had lifted him to the twentieth floor. But the butler seemed utterly unimpressed, and Fox surmised that the household staff of Irene Dunham Pomfret was hardened to apparitions from other worlds. The butler was standing by courteously while a second man in uniform, also courteously, was disposing of Fox's bag and outdoor coverings, when a woman appeared from within through a vaulted archway and approached, talking as she came.

"How do you do? I don't have any maids. I don't like them. I have only men. I had maids once, and they were always sick. You're Fox? Tecumseh Fox? I've heard a great deal about you from Diego. You were very sweet to him at the time of his misfortune. Let's go in here..."

Fox was valiantly concealing a series of shocks. The large and richly furnished reception hall had furnished one. He happened to know something about Chinese vases, through their involvement in a case he had worked on, and two rare and beautiful specimens were displayed there on a table; and on the wall back of them was an ordinary colored print of Greuze's "The Broken Pitcher"! He did not know, of course, that that had been the favorite picture of James Garfield Dunham, Mrs. Pomfret's rather sentimental first husband, nor that Mrs. Pomfret was capable of complete disregard of canons of convention and taste when her personal feelings were involved—though after one look at her the latter would have been an easy surmise.

Her appearance was the second shock. It displayed none of the bloodless and brittle insolence her reputation as a female Maecenas had led him to expect. Her figure was generous, her eyes shrewd and merry, her mouth with full lips well-disposed and satisfied with life, and her surprisingly youthful skin—considering, in view of her son Perry, that she must have been at least halfway between forty and fifty—was a flesh covering that Rubens would have enjoyed looking at. Fox himself did.

The vast chamber into which she conducted him, in which two concert grands were merely minor incidents, was overpowering but not irritating. She stopped at the edge of a priceless Zendjan rug and called in a voice that succeeded in blending tender affection with a note of command which invited instant response:

"Henry!"

A man got out of a chair and approached.

"My husband," said Mrs. Pomfret; and Fox was amazed that a woman could say that as she might have said "My airedale" or "My favorite symphony" without offending his masculine pride. She was proceeding: "This is Tecumseh Fox. I know one thing, if I were your wife and you went around with a stubble like that—"

Fox, bewildered, realeased Henry Pomfret's hand and foolishly tried to defend himself. "I had to jump and run to catch a plane and didn't have time to shave, and besides, I don't like to shave, and I haven't any wife." He glanced around, and as far as he could see there was no one else there except a girl and a young man seated on a divan. "I understood—Diego told me on the phone that you had invited everyone here who—"

"I did, but Adolph Koch sent word that he couldn't come until four o'clock, and you were on an airplane and Diego couldn't notify you—nor could my secretary reach Dora or Mr. Gill to let them know—do you know them? I suppose not."

She led the way to the divan, and the two there stood up. As Mrs. Pomfret pronounced names, Fox saw Dora's hand start up and then hesitate, and he reached for it, and found that it was shy but firm. Her cheeks were flatter than he remembered them, but, reflecting that she had just been through a severe flattening process, he was willing to concede Diego's remark about loveliness. He shook hands with Ted Gill, who had the absent and faintly resentful air of a man who had been interrupted in an agreeable and important task.

"He looks," said Mrs. Pomfret, "like a Norwegian tenor I met in Geneva in 1926 who sang with his Adam's apple."

"Not me," Henry Pomfret laughed. "I probably look to her like a crocodile she met in Egypt in 1928. That was for you, Gill."

"A cross-eyed baby crocodile," his wife retorted with fond malice. "And that Norwegian tenor, his name was— yes, Wells, what is it?"

A middle-aged man with a worried brow and harassed eyes approached. "Telephone, Mrs. Pomfret. Mr. Barbinini."

"Oh, my lord, fighting again," exclaimed Mrs. Pomfret, and rushed off.

"Will you have a drink?" offered the husband. "Dora?"

"No, thanks."

Gill declined too, but Fox admitted that he could get along with one. It appeared, however, that drinks were not available in that chamber at that hour; at any rate, Fox was conducted out of it, through another room only less large, along a corridor and around a corner, and finally into a comfortable little apartment with leather-covered chairs, a radio, books....

Pomfret went to a combination tantalus and electric refrigerator and procured necessities. Fox, glancing around, saw a Lang Yao sang-de-boeuf perched on a cabinet in a corner, and a large deep peach bloom on a table against the wall. He crossed to the latter for a closer look. Behind him Pomfret's voice inquired if he liked vases.

"I like this one," Fox declared.

"No wonder," said Pomfret with pride in his tone. "It's a Hsuan Te."

"Apparently you like them."

"I love them."

Fox glanced at him, and saw that his face, like his tone, displayed unassuming sincerity. It was even at that moment an appealing face, though he had at first sight found it not attractive, with broad mouth not harmonizing with the rather sharp nose, and the restless gray eyes too small for the brow that sloped above them.

"There's no finer peach bloom than that anywhere." Pomfret brought the drink over. "I have another one nearly as good that's in my wife's dressing room. I'll show it to you before you go, if you'd care to see it, and some others." He laughed, a bit awkwardly. "I suppose one reason I'm so proud of them is that they're the only things in the world that belong to me. It was my wife's money that bought them, of course, since I've never had any, but they're mine."

Fox sipped his highball. "What do you do, have agents on the lookout, or pick them up yourself?"

"Neither one. Not any more. I've quit. My wife doesn't like things shut up in cabinets, she likes them scattered around. For that matter, I agree with her, but about a year ago some lout knocked over a Ming five-color, the finest one I ever saw, and busted it into twenty pieces. If you'll believe it, I wept. I don't mean I sobbed, but I wept tears. That finished me. I quit. It was such a beautiful thing, and I felt responsible..."

Pomfret drank, frowned at his glass, and resumed, "Then I had another loss last fall. A Wan Li black rectangular—here, I'll show you." He put his glass down, got a portfolio from a shelf, and found a page. "Here's a color picture of it. It was absolutely unique, the gem of any collection. See that golden yellow enamel? And the green and white? But that doesn't half do it justice."

Fox scrutinized the picture. "Did it get broken too?"

"No. It was stolen. It disappeared one day when—oh well, I don't want to bore you about it."

Fox was assuring him politely that he was not at all bored when there was a knock at the door, and in response to Pomfret's invitation Perry Dunham entered.

"Orders," he stated crisply. "Checking up. Everyone's here but Koch, and Mum wanted you located." He approached Fox and extended a hand. "Hullo. I'm Perry Dunham, as you may remember from the other evening." He eyed Fox's half-empty glass. "That's an idea."

"Have one?" Pomfret offered, not, Fox thought, with excessive cordiality.

"I will if you've got bourbon."

"No bourbon, I'm sorry. Scotch, Irish, rye—"

"I'll find some bourbon." The arrogant young ape— according to Diego—departing, turned after opening the door. "Showing Mr. Fox Mum's vases? And her florins and ducats?" The door closed after him.

A patch of color appeared on the cheek of Mr. Pomfret which was visible to Fox. Apparently the emotion which caused it was for the moment too acute to be covered by conversation, and Fox, embarrassed, tried to help out.

"Picturesque," he observed lightly. "Florins and ducats?" He waved his drink. "And dinars and guineas?"

"He was referring," said Pomfret stiffly, "to a little collection of coins I have made. I took it up as a sort of consolation when I abandoned the vases. If you drop them they don't break, and even if they did it wouldn't be anything to cry about."

"Old coins? I would enjoy looking at them."

"I doubt it." Pomfret seemed considerably less enthusiastic about coins than vases as objects of prideful display. "Are you a numismatist? You mentioned dinars."

Fox said no, that "dinar" was to him only an exotic word, and that it would really be interesting to see one if there were any in the little collection. Pomfret said that he supposed they should be joining the others, but he did happen to possess a dinar of the Fatimids; and, taking a key fold from his pocket and selecting one, he opened the door of a cabinet, disclosing a tier of shelves holding rows of shallow trays. The tray he removed was partitioned into small velvet-lined compartments, in each of which reposed a coin. Pomfret pointed to one.

"That's it. Not in very good condition. This is much rarer and finer, a denier of Louis the First. That's a bonnet piece of James Fifth of Scotland. That? An old British stater—Come in!"

It was Diego Zorilla. He entered, flashed his black eyes at them, shook hands perfunctorily with Pomfret and warmly with Fox, and announced that he had been sent to fetch them. Pomfret replaced the tray and locked the cabinet. Fox swallowed the last of his drink.

"In the cathedral?" Pomfret inquired.

"No, they're in the library."

It seemed to Fox, when they got there, that the room had less right to the old-fashioned and dignified title of "library" than any he had ever seen. Some books were present, but they were lost in the indiscriminate jumble. There were racks of antique-looking musical instruments, an enormous harp, bronze and marble busts of composers, a map of the world ten feet square on which someone had painted black lines in all directions...without even starting the inventory. There were also people, seated along the sides of a large rectangular table, which gave that territory the aspect of a directors' board room, and at one end was Irene Dunham Pomfret. On her right was the harassed-looking secretary, Wells. She interrupted a conversation with Adolph Koch, on her left, long enough to call "Sit down!" to the three men arriving, without looking at them.

"They only made one of her," Diego murmured to Fox. "Once at a meeting here of the Metropolitan Symphony Board she threw the minute book at Daniel Cullen and ordered him to leave."

"There's no reason—I don't really belong—" Pomfret was saying to the length of the table.

"Sit down," said Mrs. Pomfret.

He did so, finding a place between his stepson Perry and Hebe Heath. Beyond Miss Heath was Felix Beck. Across the table, besides Fox and Diego, were Dora Mowbray, Ted Gill, and Garda Tusar, and Adolph Koch at the corner. There was talk in subdued tones. Mrs. Pomfret finished with Koch, rapped with her knuckles on the table, and the talk stopped.

She spoke with the easy and informal authority of an experienced chairwoman. "I invited you here today for two purposes. First, I think you are entitled to read the note which Jan left when—Monday evening. Or hear it read. At my suggestion the police kept it from publication, and it has been turned over to me. Let me have it, Wells."

From a portfolio on the table before him, the secretary extracted a slip of paper and handed it to her.

"It is written," she went on, "on a sheet torn from the telephone memo pad there in the dressing room, and this is what it says:

"'To my friends who believed in me. I have failed you, and I have no courage to try again. I used up all my courage during that terrible hour. That terrible sound—I tried with all my heart to make it sing and I couldn't. Dora, I don't want to say you could have made it sing if you would, but you will understand—anyway, forgive me. All of you forgive me. Really I am not going to kill myself, for I am already dead. I leave my violin to those to whom it really belongs—those who gave it to me—I had no right to it. There is nothing else for me to leave to anyone. Jan.'"

Tears started down Mrs. Pomfret's cheeks as she finished with her voice trembling. Diego growled. Felix Beck groaned, and Dora Mowbray buried her face in her hands. Garda Tusar said in a strained high-pitched voice:

"I want that paper! I want it! It's mine!"

Mrs. Pomfret, using her handkerchief on the tears, ignored her.

"I want it and I intend to have it! My brother—that was the last thing he did and I have a right to it—"

"No," said Mrs. Pomfret sharply. "You may speak to me about it later." She used her handkerchief again. "The only one mentioned by name is Dora, and if she wants to claim it she may."

"But I—"

"That will do, Garda—I'm surprised all of you don't cry. I can't read it without crying. I felt that you were entitled to know its contents, but I'm sure you will agree that they should not be publicly disclosed, especially the reference to Dora. That is a—very intimate—matter. Now—the list, Wells?"

The secretary produced another paper.

"This," Mrs. Pomfret continued, "is a list of those who contributed to the fund for the purchase of the violin:

"Lawton Mowbray ...............................................$ 1,500
Tecumseh Fox ...................................................  2,000
Hebe Heath .......................................................  2,500
Adolph Koch......................................................  10,000
Irene Dunham Pomfret.......................................  20,000

"Which makes the total $36,000, and it was possible, as you know, to get the Oksmann Stradivarius so cheaply only by a lucky chance."

"I don't see—" Adolph Koch began.

"Please, Mr. Koch. When I am through—All of you here did not contribute to that fund. I invited Dora because she is mentioned in the note, and also to represent her father's interest. If after discussion it is decided to sell the violin—I'm sure we could get what we paid for it—and return the amounts to the contributors, the $1,500 will be of great help to Dora, who is too proud and silly to accept favors from friends. I invited Garda because she is Jan's sister, Felix because he was Jan's teacher, and Diego because he was Jan's friend and was responsible for the contribution from Mr. Fox. Mr Gill came to represent Miss Heath, who said she would be unable to come, but apparently she changed her mind."

"The urgent appointment I had with important—"

"I understand, Miss Heath." Mrs. Pomfret's voice suddenly had vinegar in it. "There are some things I would like to say but can't because this is my home. I will only suggest—it will be a relief if you will leave your share of the discussion to Mr. Gill. However, before we enter upon any discussion I must tell you of a surprising—"

"What discussion?" Adolph Koch demanded. "What is there to discuss? If you mean the violin, what's the use discussing it when we don't know where it is?"

"But we do. It's here. It came this morning by parcel post, addressed to me."

Everyone stared at her except Tecumseh Fox. His eyes moved to take them all in. He saw varying degrees of surprise, interest, and the shock of the unexpected; and Hebe Heath, across the table from him, with the back of her hand pressed dramatically against her mouth, gazed in wide-eyed incredulity at her hostess.

"No!" she gasped. "You mean—Jan's violin—"

"I mean what I said," Mrs. Pomfret told her shortly.

"This is interesting," Koch murmured.

"You say it's here?" Diego rumbled. "Let's see it."

"Wells," said Mrs. Pomfret.

The secretary disappeared behind a screen, and emerged carrying a cardboard shipping carton some three feet long, which he deposited on the table in front of Mrs. Pomfret. She flipped back the folding covers and inserted her hand. Fox, shoving back his chair and starting for her, called:

"Excuse me! I wouldn't handle it."

He was at her side and met a twinkle in her eye "You mean fingerprints," she said, as to one who should be humored. "There aren't any. I asked the police commissioner to send up an expert—confidentially, of course. He wanted to take it away, but I wouldn't let him." Carefully and gently, her hand was raised from the nest of tissue paper in the carton, with all eyes staring at what it held.

"It's a violin," Koch said dryly, "but how do you know it's Jan's?"

"That's another reason I invited Felix. Felix, will you—"

Beck, already there, was reaching for it with both hands, as a woman reaches for a baby. Fox retreated a step and watched the faces; the others were watching Beck.

"It looks like it from here," Adolph Koch said to himself but audibly. He was the only one who had not left his chair; Mrs. Pomfret had stood up first, to reach into the carton. The others were stretching their necks to see, except Perry Dunham, who was so close he didn't need to, and Hebe Heath, who, her breast heaving, was clutching her throat as though to strangle intolerable suspense.

For three long minutes Felix Beck was oblivious of them. His peering intent eyes went over every inch of the beautiful golden red-brown instrument, its ancient patina now glowing, now dull, in changing angles of the light, as it was tenderly shifted in his hands. Then he held it against him, in his arms, looked at Mrs. Pomfret, and nodded.

"Well?" voices demanded in chorus.

"It's the Oksmann Stradivarius," Beck said.

A moment of complete silence was followed by noises. Perry Dunham said, "Let me see it," and stretched out a hand, but Beck continued to hug the violin. Koch muttered, "So there's something to discuss after all." Hebe Heath flopped limply into her chair. Henry Pomfret nodded his head like a man who has had surmise verified. Dora Mowbray sat down again, unsteadily, and Ted Gill followed her example if not her manner and said something to her ear. Mrs. Pomfret grasped the neck of the violin near the pegs and Beck released it, and she returned it to the nest of tissue paper.

"We may as well sit down," she said, and waited until all were back in their seats. "I think you'll agree that before we consider the question of what is to be done with it, there are one or two other points to be discussed."

"Such as," said Diego Zorilla determinedly, "whether Jan was playing on it Monday evening."

"And" put in Ted Gill, "such as who mailed it to you."

Mrs. Pomfret nodded at him. "That, I should think, comes first, but there is something else to consider even before that. The police are inclined to be interested in this—development. The man they sent here this morning wanted to take not only the violin, but also the carton and wrapper. At my request Commissioner Hombert kindly instructed him not to press the matter. After all, no crime is involved—that is, Jan did it of his own volition, if the poor boy—"

"He didn't!" The fierce exclamantion was from Jan's sister. "I don't believe it! Jan didn't kill himself! And you all know it! Some of you know it!"

"You're a fool, Garda." Perry Dunham was glaring across at her. "I was right there and saw him. So was Dora—"

"Dora!" she cried contemptuously. "You're both lying! If it hadn't been for her tricks—"

Mrs. Pomfret's palm smacked the table. "That will do,"

she said incisively. "Henry warned me that if you came you would make trouble—"

"And I will!" Garda's black eyes flashed and her voice trembled with resolve. "You can't shut me up! Just because you're Irene Dunham Pomfret! You say there was no crime—but there was! Jan was killed. He was murdered!"

A derisive snort came from Perry Dunham. His mother straightened her shoulders preparatory to commanding the unfortunate situation, but was forestalled by another voice:

"She's right." Dora Mowbray, her fingers twisted tightly together before her on the table, moved her head from side to side as though to decide which one she wanted to tell it to. "Garda's right. Jan was killed. I killed him."

4

GARDA TUSAR'S chair fell over backwards as she left it to gain her feet, but that was as far as she got, for she found her arms imprisoned in Diego Zorilla's powerful grip. Sounds from the others were overborne by that from Perry Dunham, who, his eyes popping out at Dora, barked at her across the table:

"Have you gone batty, for God's sake?"

"No, I haven't," Dora said, looking at his mother instead of him. Her voice came through a constricted throat, but there was decision in it. "I didn't know it would be like that, but I did it. I must have. I thought when the violin was gone it might have been that—but now of course it wasn't—"

"Just a minute, Miss Mowbray." Tecumseh Fox, seated at her left, addressed her profile. "Are you saying that you shot Tusar?"

Her head turned. "That I?—"

"Fired the gun. Pulled the trigger."

"Why—how could I? He did. Jan did."

"Then," Mrs. Pomfret demanded impatiently, "what are you talking about?"

"I am saying," Dora faced her again, "that I think I killed Jan. If I sound melodramatic—I don't mean to. And God knows I didn't mean him to die—I didn't even mean to hurt him—though I did before—when I thought he had killed my father—"

"Slut!" Garda spat past Diego's and Fox's faces. "It was you who started that dirty lie—"

"Garda!" Mrs. Pomfret did not spit, but her voice prevailed. "You will stop that! You will behave yourself or you'll be asked to leave, and any man here would enjoy carrying you out if it comes to that. This is disgraceful!"

Diego inquired, "Shall I?—"

"No. Put her in her chair—Now, Dora?"

"I don't blame her," Dora said. She took a deep breath. "Not that I'm a slut, nor did I start any lie. I have never said to anyone that I thought Jan killed my father, but for a time I did think so. I was—some of you know how I was—I loved my father—and I never did love Jan, the way he thought I should. And I thought I would hurt him in the only way I could hurt him."

She took another breath. "It was a vile thing even to think of, I know it was, but my father dying that way—you said yourself, Mrs. Pomfret, I was half out of my mind. I thought I would work with Jan again, practice his big concert with him, and then I would ruin it—not so anyone would know except Jan, of course. I could have done that. I thought I could, but after we had practiced a few times I realized that I couldn't—I mean that I wouldn't be able to make myself do it—and anyway, I wasn't so sure that I was right about how father died. I suppose my head was trying to get normal again."

Diego growled at her, "That wasn't a pretty idea you had, my little Dora."

"I know it, Diego. But I soon got rid of it. Anyway, I thought I had—no, I was sure of it. And Jan insisted I must work with him. Then that night came, and of course with the first bars he played I knew something was wrong, and I was afraid it was me, that I was doing unconsciously, without knowing it, what I had once planned to do. I wanted to call to him, to get up and run out, to do something, anything, but I couldn't. I had to hang on and do my best, and I did. I never tried so hard—believe me! Oh, don't you believe me? I never tried so hard—and my fingers were as stiff as my father's had been and it was all wrong—it was horrible, horrible—"

"Nonsense," Felix Beck declared gruffly. "That's all nonsense. With the piano there was nothing wrong at all. Diego, do you agree?"

"I didn't hear the piano. But I would have if there had been anything much wrong with it."

"There was," Dora insisted miserably. "There must have been! To make Jan choke it, kill it, like that? You heard him! I knew it must have been me, and when I saw him—when he—when I saw—"

"Fish!" said Mrs. Pomfret energetically. Fox darted a startled glance at her; the others, familiar with her favorite expression of impatience, merely glanced. She was going on, "Dora dear, your feeling of guilt is fantastic. Garda, your suspicions are claptrap and in extremely bad taste and you will please stop making a fool of yourself. We have a serious decision to make."

Her meeting under control, she took time to clear her throat. "As I said, the police are aware that no crime has been committed, except possibly theft, and since the violin has been returned intact they won't inquire into that unless we ask them to. So that puts it up to us. We can dispose of the violin and drop the matter, or—Garda, be quiet!—or we can have an investigation made and try to answer the questions Diego and Mr. Gill have raised, which of course were in all our minds. My own opinion is that in spite of the unpleasantness that will conceivably result from an investigation, we owe it to Jan, to ourselves, to music, to have one made." Her lips tightened. "I personally owe it to the impertinent scoundrel who sent that package to me."

Koch, frowning, inquired, "Investigation by whom?"

"The police," Garda Tusar said emphatically.

Dora Mowbray breathed, "Oh, no!" and then clasped her hand to her mouth.

"It seems to me," Hebe Heath offered, "that it would be horribly revolting—"

A sharp and commanding glance from Ted Gill silenced her, but before anyone else could speak she started again, "But, Ted, I'm sure Mr. Koch would agree, because he was saying only yesterday—you remember, Dolphie, when I asked you why nobody—"

"Hebe!" It was Ted Gill. "We're out of this."

"Very well, Ted," she said with aggrieved dignity.

"I think," said Koch, smoothly and composedly, but with a suggestion of pink on his heavy cheeks, "that it depends entirely on who does the investigating."

"So do I," Mrs. Pomfret concurred. "Luckily one of our own number—one of the present owners of the violin—is a trained and skillful investigator. Mr. Fox, will you do it?"

"Him!" Garda exploded scornfully. "One of you!"

Mrs. Pomfret, ignoring her, observed what she took for reluctance on Fox's face. "Of course," she said, "I would expect to pay you for it. Myself."

Fox shook his head. "There wouldn't be any bill." He glanced around. "If there's no objection from any of the owners of the violin—Miss Mowbray?"

Dora met his eyes, and nodded.

"Do you want me to find out what happened?"

"Yes—certainly."

"Mr. Koch?"

"By all means. An excellent idea. My knowledge of your reputation is somewhat vague—"

"I pay my income tax. Miss Heath?"

"Oh, yes!" Her tone was enthusiastic and her incredible eyes were melting under his gaze. "Please do!"

"All right, I will." Fox returned to Mrs. Pomfret. "It is understood, of course, that anything I find will be reported to all of you—I feel, as you did when you invited us here today, that consideration is due Miss Tusar and Mr. Beck and Diego. Your husband and son also, naturally."

"Thanks!" Perry Dunham said with exaggerated gratitude. "I was afraid you were going to leave me out. When and how do we start?"

Fox was out of his chair. Going to the end of the table, between Mrs. Pomfret and the secretary, he staked a claim on the carton by laying his hand on it. "I suppose," he inquired, "you kept the wrapper with the address on it? And the string?"

Mrs. Pomfret said, "Wells," and the secretary disappeared behind the screen and in a moment emerged, and handed Fox a thick fold of heavy brown wrapping paper and a neat coil of twine. Fox stuck the twine in his pocket and asked:

"It was delivered this morning?"

Wells nodded. "Around nine o'clock."

"Who opened the parcel?"

"I did. I open all packages. When I saw what was in it I informed Mrs. Pomfret immediately. We are of course not experts, but we both thought it was the Stradivarius. She instructed me to lock it in the cabinet, and she telephoned the police commissioner."

"And he sent a man to examine it for fingerprints and none were found."

"That's correct. He reported that there were none anywhere, except on the part of the wrapping paper that had been outside. And also except Mrs. Pomfret's and my own."

"Well, so much for that." Fox picked up the carton and tucked it under his arm. "Now if there's a room where I can take this for a little preliminary survey?"

"We'll leave you here with it." Mrs. Pomfret arose. "I suppose you would all like a cocktail? I know I would." She moved. "Garda, I want to talk to you. Henry, please— Henry! Miss Heath is capable of standing alone. Please tell Stevens..."

They got away from their chairs and made it a general exodus.

Fox, left to himself, set about his examination of the evidence at hand without dilation of his nostrils or any other perceptible reaction of the sort that an investigator fired with ardor is supposed to display. From his manner it might even have been suspected that at least half of his

mind was busy with something else. Not that he actually
skimped anything; he inspected with great care the violin,
the coil of string, and all sides of the carton, and then
removed methodically, one by one, the pieces of tissue
paper which had been used for packing. Apparently no
revelation appeared, for his eyes lit up with no gleam of
discovery, but they did flicker with an accent of interest
when he unfolded the sheet of wrapping paper and leaned
over to peer at the address which had been printed on it
in ink:

MRS. IRENE DUNHAM POMFRET
3070 PARK AVENUE
NEW YORK CITY

"That," he muttered, straightening up, "helps the odds
a little anyway." Noting the postmark, Columbus Circle
Station, he folded the paper up again, proceeded to repack
the carton, and, turning the cover flaps into position,
stood and drummed on them with his fingers and gazed
first at one empty chair and then at another, as if subjecting
their late occupants to a prolonged scrutiny and calculation.

The door swung open and Perry Dunham walked in.

He glanced at the closed carton and at Fox in surprise.

"What! Haven't you started the inquest yet?"

"Sure, I've finished. I'm a fast worker."

"Who sent it? Me?"

"Yes. The string smells of the perfume you use."

"Curses! Us criminals always slip up somewhere, don't
we?" The youth had crossed to Fox's end of the table.
"Mum wants to ask you something, or maybe Garda does,
anyway Mum wants you. In the yellow room, across the
big hall. She sent me to guard this while you're gone, but
in case you object you can lug it—"

"I'll take a chance, since your mother sent you. Is that
where the cocktails are?"

"Yes, but don't get fuzzy now. You're going to need all
your brains—"

Fox was going, was at the door, had it open, was in the corridor, had closed the door behind him. The entrance to this side of the big hall was twenty steps down the corridor, and he took ten of them briskly, striding along on the thick carpet, and then suddenly and abruptly turned, tiptoed swiftly back to the door he had just closed, knelt, and put his eye to the keyhole. One glance sufficed; in one burst of movement he flung the door open and regained his feet across the threshold.

The flaps of the carton were open, tissue was scattered on the table, and Perry Dunham, startled fury on his face, stood at the edge of the screen with the violin in his hands.

"Goddam you," Perry said through his teeth.

"And how about you?" Fox moved forward, not in haste. As he got to the far end of the table and approached Perry, the young man drew back a step, clutching the violin, his body tensed for resistance, his face pale and defiant.

"Relax," Fox said curtly. "Hand it over."

Perry retreated another step. "Listen—"

"I'm deaf. I may be able to hear you when that thing is back where it belongs."

Perry obviously did not intend to put it back where it belonged. He intended to fight. That was in his eyes, and it remained in them for ten seconds while they withstood Fox's steady relentless gaze. Then they flickered, wavered....

"We can't roughhouse," he said. "We'd bust it. You don't want to bust it."

"I'll take a chance if you start going anywhere. I can stand here as long as you can."

The two pairs of eyes met and clashed again, and then suddenly Perry held out the violin and Fox took it.

"Now," Fox said, "I can hear better if you care to explain—"

Perry laughed shortly and not agreeably. "How would you like to go to hell? If only this had been somewhere else! If only..." He shrugged it off. "I'll drown it in bourbon." He tramped out, disappearing through the open door without bothering to close it.

Fox put the violin to bed again, placing the wrapping paper on top of the tissue before closing the flaps, got the carton snugly under his arm, and departed—down the corridor, across the main hall, where a man directed him to the yellow room, and into the presence of the hostess and the remaining guests. A glance showed him that they were all there with the exceptions of Hebe Heath and Ted Gill, in more or less animated conversation over cocktails. He crossed to where Mrs. Pomfret sat with Garda Tusar:

"Excuse me. Did you want to speak to me?"

"I?" She looked blank. "Oh. My son suggested—we were trying to persuade Garda to be reasonable—and he thought you might do that more effectively than we could—"

"I'll be glad to try, though not right now." Fox, glancing from her to meet Garda's black eyes, saw no great promise of reasonableness there, though there was no lack of other qualities which might be admired and responded to by anyone with an inclination that way.

Mrs. Pomfret, glancing at the bulky carton under his arm, inquired, "Do you want Wells to lock that up again?"

"No, thanks." Fox turned. Conversation had stopped and he had all the eyes. Wells and Felix Beck were off in a corner, Henry Pomfret and Dora were on a nearby divan, Diego and Adolph Koch were standing in the middle of the room. Backed up to a window, with a drink in his hand, Perry Dunham met Fox's gaze with a cool stare.

"I'm going," Fox announced, "and I'm taking this with me. I'll take good care of it. As soon as there is something worth reporting, I'll report it. If I need to consult with any of you individually, which is probable, I'll get in touch with you through Wells." He moved.

"Have you got the violin in there?" Koch asked.

"I have."

"Don't you think it would be safer—"

"I think," said Fox from the door, "that it's safer with me than it would be—anywhere else."

# 5

"YOU'VE GOT me wrong," Ted Gill said earnestly. "Honest you have. I don't regard myself as a whizz-bang."

He was seated on an Empire bench with carved legs, with his back to the keyboard of a concert grand piano. It was Saturday afternoon. The piano occupied a good quarter of the space in a walk-up room-and-bath on the third floor of a brick building in the Sixties east of Lexington Avenue, and the rest of the furniture looked equally out of place. But when, upon the sudden death of a girl's widower father, she finds that all she owns in the world is the contents of her own room in his elaborate apartment on 57th Street which has been her home, what is to be done? As for the piano, that was for Dora Mowbray a necessity, since without it giving lessons to little boys and girls would have been impossible.

Dora, sitting on a chair that Caruso had once sat on, holding her, a three months' baby, in his arms, had a flush on her cheeks which did no harm to her appearance. Nor, for that matter, did the faint wrinkle on her brow which gave her eyes an intentness to match the earnestness of the young man who faced her.

"You certainly do," she said with spirit. "Not that I don't admire a good piece of bravura, but you pile it on so. Why don't you carry cymbals?" The flush was spreading. "Please don't stare at me like that!"

"I'm not staring. I'm just looking." Ted, already on the edge of the bench, came forward another inch. "Look here, I might as well confess something. That was bunk about my wanting to plug you for radio. I wanted to come—I had to see you—and I couldn't—" He was floundering. "Damn it," he said resentfully, "when I'm

41

talking to you I can't even make a sentence with a subject
and predicate! You might think if I wanted to see you I
could just have told you on the phone that I wanted to see
you!"

"Yes, you might," Dora agreed. "Why didn't you?"

"Because I was afraid you wouldn't let me come! Not
only do you have a funny effect on my grammar, you've
turned me into a coward! Oh no, I had to think up
something fancy for an excuse! That would have been
understandable if I had just wanted to come because I like
to look at you and hear you and be near you...."

He was suddenly redder than she was. He slid back on
the bench and said in a determined voice, "But I had to
see you because I had to tell you something. It was me
that mailed that violin to Mrs. Promfret."

Dora's mouth fell open.

"It was me," Ted repeated firmly. "I wrapped it up and
addressed it and mailed it to her."

"Good lord," Dora said dully.

"I nearly told them about it yesterday afternoon, there
at Mrs. Pomfret's, but I decided not to. Because I doubt if
it would really help them any to know, but that's what I
want to ask you. I'll do whatever you say. If you think I
ought to tell them, I will."

"But I don't understand." The flush had gone from
Dora's cheeks, leaving them pallid. "If that's Jan's violin—
then it was you who took it...."

"No, it wasn't. But I see now that I have to tell you that
too. I thought maybe—"

"You don't have to tell me anything." Dora's lip started
to quiver and she put her teeth on it.

"You think I don't?" Ted was getting to his feet, then he
dropped back onto the bench again, looking helpless. "For
the love of Mike, don't look like that. That's the way you
looked the first time I saw you that Monday night—kind
of, I don't know, brave and beautiful—like that. I thought I
was a grown man, I ought to be, I'm thirty years old, but I
don't know, when I look at you...Listen to me now, I
came here to tell you a certain sapific thing—I mean a
specific thing—"

A bell rang. Ted stopped short.

"That was a bell ringing," he said.

"Yes," Dora said. "My doorbell." She didn't move. "I don't know who would be—"

"They'll go away." Ted was imploring. "Why not just let 'em go away?"

The bell rang again.

"Oh!" Dora sprang to her feet. "I forgot! Mr. Fox! He phoned not long after you did and said he wanted to see you and couldn't find you and asked if I knew where you were—and I said you were coming here—and he asked if he could come and I said he could—"

"That bird," Ted said gloomily. His eyes appealed to her. "He can go away as well as anybody else."

Dora shook her head. "I couldn't do that. He was nice to me." She was moving toward a button on the wall. "Anyway, he knows we're—I'm here—"

"Wait a minute." Ted went to her, faced her. "Listen." He swallowed. "What I told you about the violin—I'm not sure they'll have to know. It would be, uh, embarrassing. So if you wouldn't mention it to Fox? Please?"

The bell rang.

Dora's questioning eyes slanted up under her troubled frown and met his, beseeching.

"Please?" he begged. "I came here to tell you about it, and I'm going to, and I'll do whatever you think I ought to."

Dora nodded uncertainly, turned from him to push the button, and opened the door to the hall. In a moment Ted's voice sounded behind her:

"Yep, that's him all right. That's the way he would come up stairs. My God, he's sprightly."

Dora did not know that her manner of shaking hands with Tecumseh Fox at their first meeting, the day before at Mrs. Pomfret's, was chiefly responsible for his being nice to her, so there could have been no artifice in its repetition now—the impulsive friendly offer halted abruptly in mid-air as if uncertain of its welcome. Fox, ready for it this time, had his hand already there. Ted Gill, having retreated within, was not seen until the other two had entered; he acknowledged Fox's greeting with an uncivil grunt, watched the disposal of his hat and coat with a sullen eye, and, when Dora sat down, replanted himself firmly on the piano bench. He spoke as one in a hurry to get something disposed of:

"Miss Mowbray says that you phoned that you were looking for me. Can I do something for you?"

"Yes, if you don't mind," Fox took some papers from his pocket, thumbed through them and selected one, unfolded it and glanced at it. "I thought it would save time to write this out and have it ready for you to sign." He extended the paper in his hand and Ted took it.

As Ted read, the others watched his face. At the first glance his brows were raised, then they came down to participate in a frown of astonishment. His lips parted, then his jaws snapped them shut. Finally he looked at Fox, plainly flabbergasted, and then got up and handed the paper to Dora.

"Read that, will you?" he requested plaintively. She glanced up at him, at Fox, and then looked at the paper:

*I, Theodore Gill, hereby declare and affirm:*

*That on Thursday afternoon, March 7th, 1940, Hebe Heath admitted to me that on the preceding Monday evening she had removed Jan Tusar's violin from his dressing room at Carnegie Hall, and taken it to her rooms at the Churchill Hotel, and that it was still in her possession. She also told me that it had been locked in her wardrobe trunk continuously from Monday night until that moment.*

*That I advised her to return the violin immediately to its owners (a group of five persons of whom she is one). That she asked my assistance. That I procured a carton, wrapping paper, tissue and string, packed the violin, addressed the package to Mrs. Irene Dunham Pomfret, and mailed it.*

*That the violin taken by Miss Heath from her trunk, in my presence, is the one I sent to Mrs. Pomfret, and I am firmly convinced, from what Miss Heath told me, that it is the one she took from Tusar's dressing room Monday evening.*

"I see," Dora said. Her voice sounded strained. "Naturally you would want to protect Miss Heath—"

"Nothing doing," Ted declared incisively. "Oh, no. This is bad enough as it is, without any misunderstanding on that score. Naturally I would want to strangle Miss Heath. But a publicity agent who obeyed his natural impulses would be in jail in five minutes. One of my colleagues in Hollywood..." He shrugged, and turned to stare at Fox. "You seem to be pretty stupendous. How come?"

Fox smiled at him. "Will you sign it?"

"I will if you'll tell me how the devil you got onto it."

"Nothing very adroit. Not at all stupendous. Miss Heath left the scene alone and in a hurry that evening, and was wearing a wrap that might easily have concealed the violin. Item two, I have never seen anything as hammy as her performance yesterday when Mrs. Pomfret announced that she had received the violin by parcel post—the back of her hand to her mouth and her eyes popping out and gasping for breath. The very essence of ham. Item three, the IRENE in the address on the package. Started to make a B and changed it to an N. Might have been thinking of Hebe."

"I was thinking of her all right," Ted declared grimly.

"No doubt. Of course it wasn't conclusive, but it was enough to suggest a call on Miss Heath. I was with her an hour—one of the most singular hours in my experience. You should be able to tell me: Which is she, subtler than a serpent or not quite brainy?"

"I can tell you," Ted said emphatically.

"Please do."

"Between you and me and Miss Mowbray."

"Certainly."

"Well. It's hard to find words. She is dumb beyond all previous manifestations of dumbness. Beyond the wildest dream of hebetude. Dumb enough to chew on the stick instead of sucking the lollipop. Dumb enough to grab a violin and scram for absolutely no reason whatever except that the violin's there and she has fingers to pick it up with and an ermine wrap to hide it under."

Fox was frowning. "That's a little hard to take. That last one. I'm a little partial to motives."

"You were with her an hour," Ted expostulated. "Where do motives originate? In the heart. Okay, say she has a heart. What is necessary for a motive to result in action? Transference through a nervous center called a brain. Well?"

"Maybe," Fox conceded doubtfully. "Anyway, we'll leave it at that for the present. May I have that paper, Miss Mowbray? Thank you." He took his pen from his pocket and offered it to Ted. Ted spread the paper on the piano arm and wrote his name below the statement, as illegibly as possible, blew on it to dry it, and handed it over.

"Much obliged." Fox stuck it in his pocket. "Another little point. Would you mind telling me what you and Miss Heath were doing in Tusar's dressing room Monday evening? I mean before the concert."

"Why didn't you ask her?"

"I did. She said something about music being sublime. She pronounced it—"

"I know how she pronounces it. We went there to ask Tusar to have his picture taken with Miss Heath, with her holding the violin, and he refused. Miss Heath began to undergo emotions, and Tusar walked out."

Fox nodded. "I saw him." He turned to Dora. "May I ask you, Miss Mowbray, did Tusar practice with you Monday afternoon?"

Dora shook her head. "Not in the afternoon. I went to his studio in the morning and we went through the Saint-Saens piece three times, but not the others. I left a little after twelve and didn't see him again until evening, at the hall."

"Why did you go through it three times? Didn't it sound right?"

"I thought it did, but Jan wasn't satisfied, especially with the animato after the introduction and the last eight measures before the allegro begins. He said he was racing it—"

"But the violin was all right? The tone? It didn't sound as it did that evening?"

"Good heavens, no. In the evening it was terrible. From the very beginning it was terrible—but you heard it...."

"Yes, I heard it." Fox arose and went to get his coat. "I'll run along. Thank you very much."

"So it's all—all over." Dora moved toward the door. "It was Jan's violin, and there was nothing—and that's all."

"Not all, Miss Mowbray." Fox got his other arm in. "I've answered the questions you folks gave me, but I've run up against another one, and I'm afraid it's a good deal uglier than those."

"Uglier?..." she faltered.

"Yes. You'll be hearing from Mrs. Pomfret, asking you to be there tomorrow at two o'clock. You too, Gill. In the meantime, you might be considering whether driving a man to suicide can be called murder. It's a nice point."

# 6

THE TENDENCY of the human animal to follow a pattern, however recently molded, was illustrated on Sunday afternoon in Mrs. Pomfret's library. Those twelve people had gathered there and sat at that table only once before, but as Mrs. Pomfret's glance went down one side and up the other, she noted that each occupied the same chair as on the previous occasion. At her left Adolph Koch, and beyond him Ted Gill, Dora Mowbray, Tecumseh Fox, Diego Zorilla and Garda Tusar; at her right was Wells, then her son, her husband, Hebe Heath and Felix Beck. The meeting had convened a little late, for Fox had not arrived until a quarter past two. That must have been intentional, since he invariably got to places well ahead of time.

Mrs. Pomfret, completing her regnant glance, said that Mr. Fox had a report to make, and nodded at him.

Fox took a paper from his pocket, announced, "This is a statement signed yesterday by Mr. Theodore Gill," and read it aloud.

The reactions were varied and in two quarters spectacular: Perry Dunham burst into a roar of laughter, and Hebe Heath, after maintaining a haughty stare at Fox until he reached the end, suddenly covered her face with her beautiful hands and moaned. Ted Gill glared across at her; Garda's eyes were flashing daggers; Henry Pomfret, next on her left, moved to increase the space between them. Diego Zorilla muttered in astonishment:

"A woman of course—but that one?" He demanded of Fox, "What is it, then? Merely a devil in her?"

Felix Beck was finding his tongue. "You!" he blurted. "I warned him! I warned Jan many times about you—"

"This is drivel," Adolph Koch said sharply. "To begin with, I should like to know why Mr. Gill signed so extraordinary—"

"It is not drivel!" Garda cut him off. "She's a Nazi!"

"Good God," Ted Gill murmured in stupefaction.

"You, Garda," Koch said caustically, "are an imbecile."

"Oh, I am?" Garda was bitter, sarcastic, and triumphant. "I am always an imbecile, you think? When I said Jan was murdered I was an imbecile? So you said." She snapped open her handbag, fumbled in it with hasty fingers, and took out an envelope. "This came to me today. Read it and see what you think now."

Diego, next to her, had a hand there for it, but she reached around him toward Fox. Fox took the envelope, glanced at the address and postmark, extracted a slip of paper and looked at it front and back.

"No salutation," he announced. "Hand-printed in ink— not, by the way, the same hand as on the package sent to Mrs. Pomfret—and it says: 'Those who seek to damage the Reich will suffer for it as your brother did. Heil

Hitler!' Below, for signature, is a swastika. You say you got this today, Miss Tusar?"

"Yes. This morning by special delivery."

"I noticed the special delivery. May I keep it?"

"No. I'm going to give it to the police."

"As you please, of course. But I'd like to discuss it with you later—"

"Discuss it now," Koch said bluntly. "It's ridiculous! The idea that Miss Heath is a Nazi—What do you say to that, Mr. Gill?"

"Nothing. I'm petrified."

"It's absurd. Nor does that swastika thing prove that Nazis were responsible for Jan's death; they may merely be taking credit for a misfortune they had nothing to do with."

"Anyhow," Mrs. Pomfret put in, "since Garda insists on turning it over to the police, that's out of our hands. But I think the statement Mr. Gill signed entitles us to an explanation from Miss Heath. For what purpose did she remove the violin from the dressing room and keep it concealed for two days?"

Ted Gill groaned.

"That," Fox said, "can wait. Any of you may ask Miss Heath about it later if you find it worth while. It is Mr. Gill's opinion that, seeing the violin there, she surrendered to an irrational and irresistible impulse."

"I don't believe it," Mrs. Pomfret said flatly.

"Well," Perry Dunham offered, "here's a suggestion that may solve two mysteries at once. I doubt if she's a Nazi, but what if she's a kleptomaniac?" He grinned crookedly at his stepfather. "She was here the day your Wan Li vase was stolen, wasn't she? I'll bet she swiped it, maybe starting a collection. Then she swiped the violin to start another collection—"

"Do you," Koch inquired acidly of Mrs. Pomfret, "approve of your son's brand of humor, madam?"

She met his gaze and matched his tone. "I don't regard it as humor, Mr. Koch. However he may have meant it. The same idea had occurred to me, quite seriously. When the vase disappeared you may remember that you said, of course in jest, that you must have taken it yourself because you were the only one present who appreciated its beauty and value. Though my husband and I have suspected Miss Heath all along, we have naturally kept silent, since there has been no evidence. Now we may at least say what we think. You agree, Henry?"

"I suppose so." Pomfret looked uncomfortable. "If it will do any good. If it will get the vase back..."

"It may have that result." Mrs. Pomfret aimed her shrewd eyes at Fox. "Will you please tell us how you learned that it was Miss Heath who stole the violin?"

"No," Fox said bluntly. "At least not now, because I have something more important to tell you. We've been investigating what happened to the violin after Tusar used it Monday evening. Now the question is, what happened to it before he used it?"

There was an edge to his voice, a warning mordacity, that fastened all eyes on him.

"Or rather," he went on, "the question is, who did it, because I know what happened. At some time between Monday noon and eight o'clock that evening, someone poured a lot of varnish through one of the f-holes and tilted the violin around to spread it over the inside of the back."

There were ejaculations of incredulity and astonishment.

"God almighty," Felix Beck said. "But that—no one alive—" He stopped, stunned.

"I discovered it," Fox continued, "when I inserted a pencil flash through an f-hole. I could see only a portion of the inside, so I don't know whether it's spread all over or not, but probably it is. I scraped some out with a stick, and it's still gummy, so it hasn't been there long. I consulted an expert—"

"Where is it?" Adolph Koch demanded.

"As I said, on the inside—"

"No, I mean the violin. Where's the violin?"

"It's in a bank vault. You may take my word for it that the varnish is there. An expert told me that it may be permanently ruined. It can be unboarded and the varnish removed, but it has probably soaked into the wood fibers enough to alter the tone even if that is done. He also told me that a thick coat of varnish on the inside of either the back or the belly would destroy the resonance and brilliance of any fine violin, and that anyone familiar with musical instruments would know that."

He looked around at them, his penetrating gaze halting a moment at each face; and when it reached Hebe Heath, she, choosing that juncture to contribute a grotesquerie which under more favorable circumstances would have got her the entire audience, pressed her palms to her breasts and exclaimed in a hollow and dreadful tone:

"Varnish!"

But no one seemed to hear it. Each in his turn and his own way was meeting the challenge of Fox's silent survey. He broke the silence and spoke to all:

"So you have it, and you don't like it. I don't blame you. I suppose Miss Tusar regards this as confirming her suspicion that her brother was murdered. Perhaps. Perhaps not, legally. Whoever ruined his violin may merely have intended to humiliate and disgrace him. Even if it was calculated that in his distress Tusar would kill himself, it would be difficult, if not impossible, to prove that the calculation existed and led to premeditated murder. So I doubt if anyone is going to pay for Tusar's life with his own. But some kind of payment is going to be made. When I sat in that auditorium Monday evening and watched Tusar's face I didn't know what was going on, but I do now, and though I've dealt with a lot of crime professionally, including murder, I don't remember anything quite as damnable and devilish as that."

"Is your tone," Koch inquired caustically, "intended to rebuke our moral palsy? I assure you I didn't pour varnish in Jan's violin."

There were mutterings. Fox said sharply. "A rebuke is none of my business, but the facts are. I am no longer making a friendly report to a group of which I am a member. I am going to do one of two things immediately: either I shall question each of you in turn privately and thoroughly, and you will answer—"

"Fish! Mrs. Pomfret said emphatically. "We certainly have to decide what's to be done, but if you think you're going to turn my house into a police station—"

"That's the alternative, Mrs. Pomfret. The police, or me. Moreover, I'll start with your son. When I was left alone here the other day, he came and said you wanted me. He stayed here, I went out, but I doubled back and looked through the keyhole, and he had pawed into the package and got the violin. If you had seen his face when I entered, and heard what he said, you would have known as I did that he wasn't merely passing the time."

Eyes went to Perry Dunham. Mrs. Pomfret, frowning at Fox in disbelief, opened her mouth and closed it again, and then turned to her son and asked quietly, "What is this, Perry?"

"Nothing, Mum." The young man reached across Wells to pat the back of her hand. "You know me, always up to mischief. I was going to plant a clue for him."

Fox shook his head. "You'll have to do a lot better than that before we're through." He stood up. "If the rest of you will please leave me here with Mr. Dunham? Since it's Sunday afternoon, I don't suppose any of you have important engagements. If you have, and must leave before I get to you, I would like to see you as soon as possible. When I finish here I may or may not report to the police. That will depend."

Hesitantly, with glances and murmurs, they pushed back their chairs. Koch addressed Fox:

"You said the varnish was put in the violin between noon Monday and eight in the evening. How do you know that?"

"Because the tone was all right when Tusar finished practicing with Miss Mowbray at noon."

"How do you justify your assumption that one of us did it?"

"Not my assumption. I make a start here, that's all."

Most of them had started for the door, but were lingering. Mrs. Pomfret had moved to confront Fox:

"I'm going to have a few words with my son. I'll send him back here as soon as I'm through. This high-handed procedure—I presume you are aware that your threat to go to the police is a gross breach of our confidence in your discretion?"

"I don't regard it so." Fox met her gaze. "And I meant what I said. I wish to question your son immediately."

"So do I. And I intend to. I would advise you, Mr. Fox—"

"Take me first," Henry Pomfret interceded from behind her elbow. "That is, if I'm included—"

"Attaboy," Perry Dunham cackled. "Hurling yourself into the front line—"

"Come, Perry." Mrs. Pomfret had her son's arm.

"But, Mum, I assure you—"

"You come with me. Henry, I approve of your suggestion. Stay with Mr. Fox. If he wishes to search the house for cans of varnish, by all means let him."

She marched out with her son in tow. The others had gone. Perry, as he pulled the door to behind him, stuck his face beyond its edge to grimace derisively at the two who were left.

Henry Pomfret seated himself in the chair Diego Zorilla had vacated. Fox scowled down at him through a moment's silence and then declared: "For a lead nickel I'd use that phone now."

Pomfret nodded. "If I were in your place that's what I would do." He added hastily, "But I hope you won't. Naturally you resent my wife's taking Perry off like that, but that's how she does things. She called you highhanded, and she doesn't realize she's highhanded herself. She can't help it. She was rich before she married Dunham, and ten times richer when he died, and you know what money does to people, even the best of them, and she's one of the best."

Fox turned a chair around, sat down, and, resting his chin on his thumb, regarded the husband speculatively. The face he saw irritated him. Yet there was nothing especially disagreeable about nature's silly attempt to compose a human countenance out of a broad mouth and a sharp nose, small gray eyes and a wide sloping brow. Was he then irritated, not by what he saw, but by what he knew, that this man lived on his wife's money? That suspicion, that he was allowing an appraisal to be adulterated by a prejudice, and a herd prejudice at that, provoked him further. He abandoned the appraisal and inquired abruptly:

"Why did you and your wife leave before the concert began Monday evening?"

Pomfret blinked. Then he smiled wryly. "Well," he said, "I left because she told me to take her home."

"Why did she want to go home? Hadn't she gone there to attend the concert?"

"Yes. That was the intention." Pomfret leaned back in his chair and folded his arms. "You know, you're putting me on a sort of spot. No doubt the proper thing is to tell you that if you want to know why my wife left before the concert you can ask her, but if you did ask her she would as likely as not tell you to go to the devil, and then you might attach undue importance to something wholly trivial. On the other hand, if I tell you and she finds out that I did…" He shrugged. "That seems to be the lesser evil. It was a tactical retreat. The Briscoe-Pomfret War."

"War?"

"My lord, you've never even heard of it?" Pomfret was amazed. "But then, you aren't living in the trenches, as I am. Mrs. Briscoe is short on matériel, meaning money, compared to my wife, so she adopts a guerilla technique. She snipes. Last year, for instance, she practically kidnapped Glissinger, the pianist. Not long ago she coerced a promise from Jan to play at a musical for her. My wife talked him out of it. Monday evening in his dressing room he blurted at her that he had reconsidered and was going to keep his promise. Just before his concert was no time to start a counterattack, so she merely went home. The fact is, she has been damned upset about it, though she would never admit it. She thought her running out on his concert might have been responsible for the way he played, just as Dora thought it might have been her fault. Now you say it was something more deliberate—and a lot more damnable. God knows I agree, if it happened the way you think it did."

"How else could it have happened?"

"I don't know." Pomfret, looking uncomfortable, hesitated. "You're experienced at this kind of thing and I'm not. But you said the varnish was put in the violin between noon and eight o'clock Monday, and frankly, I don't see how you can be sure of that."

"Do you mean it might have been done after the concert? During the two days it was in Miss Heath's possession?"

"Well—you can't rule it out as impossible, can you?"

"I can rule it out as silly," Fox declared shortly. "If the varnish wasn't in it Monday evening, what was wrong with it? Why wasn't it all right? If you like to suppose Miss Heath put the varnish in, why not suppose she did it before the concert instead of after?"

Pomfret flushed. "I don't," he said stiffly, "particularly like to suppose Miss Heath did it. If what my wife said about my vase made you think I'm ill-disposed toward Miss Heath, you're wrong. I have never thought it likely that she took the vase."

"Your wife said that both of you have suspected her all along."

"My wife has. I'm not responsible for her interpretation of my failure to fly to Miss Heath's defense. Ordinary common sense would keep a man from defending a beautiful young woman against his wife's suspicion."

Fox considered that, and disposed of it by remarking, "I'm not married." If the fact was regarded by him as a cause for regret, he successfully excluded it from his tone. He went on, "There, in Tusar's dressing room, you said he blurted something at your wife. Was there a scene?"

"I wouldn't say a scene. No. But there was certainly an atmosphere. Jan always had nerves, but I had never seen him so much on edge. My wife knew what that concert meant to him, and she tried to calm him down."

"How long were you in there?"

"Oh, ten minutes, perhaps fifteen."

"Was there anyone else there?"

"Yes. Perry went in with us, but his mother told him to go and look up Dora. Beck went with him. Mrs. Briscoe was there. She's a damn fool, and it was her mentioning her musical that made Jan say what he did to my wife."

"Did she leave the dressing room before you did?"

"I don't..." Pomfret thought a moment. "Yes, I do, she went out with Koch and left us in there. Or rather, Koch took her out. Koch was already there when we arrived."

"Was there anyone else in there while you were? Perry, Beck, Mrs. Briscoe, Koch. Anyone else?"

I think not. I'm sure not. Just as we left Miss Heath and that fellow Gill went in."

"Where was the violin?"

"The violin? I don't remember—" Pomfret checked himself, frowned, and breathed. "Oh," he said. "I see. You think it may have been done right there in the dressing room. I suppose that's possible. There were a lot of people around, but of course they weren't especially noticing the violin. It must have been there, but I don't remember seeing it."

"Soon after you left, Tusar appeared at the door of the dressing room and had it in his hand."

"Well, it wasn't in his hand while I was there. I'm sure I would have noticed it if it had been."

"When was the last time you had seen Tusar prior to that evening at the hall?"

"I saw him Monday afternoon."

Fox's brows went up. "You did?"

"Yes." Pomfret moved in his chair and an embarrassed little laugh escaped him. "So if you're going by the law of averages you'll probably pick me for the varnish suspect, or my wife, because we both had two opportunities. Only it happens that I didn't see the violin either time. We were at the Garden at a matinee, a skating ballet, and we dropped in at Jan's studio a little after five to invite him to have tea with us."

"Did he accept?"

"He didn't get invited. Diego and Koch were there, and my wife isn't particularly fond of Koch. We stayed perhaps a quarter of an hour and then—What's that?"

Pomfret jerked erect in his chair to rigid attention. Fox

turned his head, ears alert, listened, and turned back again:

"It sounded like a female scream. Someone probably spilled a drink on Miss Heath—"

But Pomfret was on his feet. "Not Miss Heath—I think—"

A bellow came, from a distance and through the door, an urgent resounding bellow, in the bass of Diego Zorilla:.

"Fox! *Fox!*"

Fox bounded across to the door, jerked it open, and was in the hall; and saw Diego headed for him on the run, with an expression on his face that no drink spilled on Hebe could have accounted for. He braked to a stop.

"Well?" Fox demanded.

"Old Stony Face," Diego rumbled. "Overlook my excitement. I beg your pardon. I think he's dead." He hooked a thumb back over his shoulder. "In there. Would you care to look?"

As Fox moved forward, Henry Pomfret, on a gallop, shot past him; and by the time he had traversed the corridor and reception hall and entered the yellow room, Pomfret had already reached his wife and had an arm around her shoulder, as she leaned against a lacquered table telling the transmitter of a yellow enameled telephone, in a tone more hollow and dreadful than anything Hebe Heath could have produced:

"...Doctor Corbett, at once...."

Other voices, commotion, servants running....

Fox pushed through the huddled guests and knelt beside a prostrate motionless figure on the floor.

# 7

THE OUTRAGED and inquisitive law closed in.

The phone call went to the 19th precinct at 3:36 P.M. At 3:40 a radio car arrived, and at 3:42 a second one. One

minute later came a precinct lieutenant with two men; all
three entered the building, but shortly the two men
emerged onto the sidewalk again and joined a colleague in
uniform who was engaged in a heated argument with a
woman in a fur coat who was in the driver's seat of a black
sedan drawn up at the curb twenty yards from the entrance to 3070. One of the men energetically dispersed a
small crowd of kibitzers that had collected and commanded
them to move on; the other, after a short contribution to
the argument, climbed to the roof of the sedan, perched
there on his knees inspecting a spot near its center, bent
over to sniff at it, and straightened to call down:

"Go get a blotter inside there!"

"Get it yourself!" his comrade retorted from the pavement. "I'm finding pieces of glass!" As in fact he was.

At 3:49 a carload of reinforcements, not in uniform,
arrived. One took over the argument with the woman in
the fur coat; a second clambered to the sedan's roof to
consider the problem presented there; the others scattered
to look for pieces of glass and shoo onlookers away. A
limousine which tried to approach was held off and tenants
of 3070, though enveloped in mink, were ruthlessly compelled to walk an extra thirty steps with no canopy to protect
them in case it had suddenly started to rain. At four
o'clock another police car swerved to the curb and a man
with a black bag got out and hurried into the building. At
4:08 still another arrived and disgorged five men with a
variety of kits and paraphernalia; and two minutes later, at
4:10, the chief of staff himself appeared. Followed by two
subordinates, he descended from his car in the middle of
the street, walked over and accosted a man standing by
the black sedan:

"What's all this?"

"A bottle of whisky thrown from a window up there,
Inspector. Hit the top of this car and broke. We've gathered
up all we can find, and we got a little of the liquid with a
medicine dropper—"

"All right, hold everything until I get a look upstairs.
Apologize to the lady—"

"Yes, sir, I am. She's going to report me and see the mayor and sue the city..."

But Inspector Damon of the Homicide Squad had moved on. A large loose-jointed man, with the jaw of a prizefighter and the morose eyes of a pessimistic poet, he did not appear, as he strode into the lobby and headed for the elevators, to feel with an intensity the outrage of the law at finding itself flouted, but in fact he was outraged. Familiar as he was with crime, and willing to accept it as a necessary element in the composition of the metropolitan scene, after twenty years on the New York police force, he was always affronted by its insolent and improper intrusion into circles where it did not belong. So when he entered the richly furnished Pomfret reception hall and accepted the offer of a uniformed policeman to take his hat and coat, he was not only an officer of the law performing his duty, but also a man with a personal grievance. He scowled at a bulk approaching from the right and inquired testily, "Where's Craig?"

And when he had been conducted into a large chamber with yellow paneled walls and yellow furniture, and across to the far side, he stood and frowned down in silence at a figure stretched out on the floor. A man kneeling there twisted his neck to look up at him, nodded a greeting, returned articles to a black bag that was open beside him, and got to his feet. The inspector turned to another man who had detached himself from a group in the middle of the room, and demanded:

"Well?"

Sergeant Craig looked as if he too felt that crime had its place and it was not here. "It's about as bad as you could ask for, Inspector," he said gloomily. "Dead on arrival. Perry Dunham, son of Mrs. Pomfret. Drank whisky with eight other people in the room and collapsed and had convulsions and died. No statement, nothing. The doctor says cyanide poisoning."

"I said indicated," the man with the bag interjected. "I'm not going to have—"

"Thank *you*," Damon said with peevish sarcasm; and

knelt beside the figure on the floor, supported himself with his hands, lowered his face until his nose was all but touching the lips which had recently belonged to Perry Dunham, and sniffed. After another sniff he straightened, scrambled to his feet, started to brush off his knees from force of habit but desisted when he saw there was no need for it, turned to Sergeant Craig and demanded:

"Who the hell threw a bottle of whisky out of the window?"

"I don't know, sir, we only got here a couple of minutes ago. Lieutenant Wade of the Nineteenth—"

"Right here, Inspector," came a voice from a man entering. He advanced briskly. "Arrived at 3:43. Dead on arrival. Four radio men were already here. I was told a whisky bottle had been thrown from a window—"

"Who threw it?"

"I don't know. There were ten people here to handle, not counting three or four servants, and all I know is Tecumseh Fox told me—"

"Fox! How the devil did he get here?"

"He didn't get here, he was here."

"Where is he?"

"In yonder. A room they call the library. I herded them all out of here and got names and addresses." The lieutenant offered a sheet of paper. "That's as far as I've got, except that I got the glass Dunham drank out of just before he went down. I gave it to Sergeant Craig."

Damon ran his eye down the list of names and up again, grunted, and turned to the sergeant. "All right, get busy. Give it the works. I want what you find in the pockets. As soon as you have pictures of it send it down for a p.m. Find something that had the poison in it—it could have been either a liquid or a powder. Smell for cyanide and remember the powder doesn't smell till you wet it. They think they've got something down below in a medicine dropper. Get it down to the laboratory, and pieces of the bottle they've collected, and that glass he drank out of. Keep two men on the door. Doctor, I'd appreciate a p.m. report as soon as possible."

"Sunday afternoon," the doctor said dismally.

"Yeah, it's Sunday where I am too. All right, Lieutenant, where's the library and for God's sake quit looking as if someone poisoned this fellow just to give you a break and get your name in the paper."

"This way, Inspector," said the lieutenant in a dignified tone.

Inside the library door, Inspector Damon stopped, looked around, heaved a sigh, and looked around again. Fifteen faces had turned to him as he entered, and even with the little he already knew it was barely this side of certainty that back of one of those pairs of eyes was a brain desperately rallying all its cunning and courage for defense against a deadly peril. It was the way some murderers comported themselves when menaced by the deadly peril which he represented that gave the inspector a high opinion of the mental and nervous equipment of men and women; he was still capable of amazement that so cureless a guilt could preserve itself silent and unseen in the tiny prison of a human skull....

"Mrs. Pomfret," Lieutenant Wade said.

She was approaching, and Damon moved to meet her. "I'm Inspector Damon," he said gruffly, feeling awkward. He was no stranger to the ordinary extravagances of grief and could deal with them without much discomfort, but this woman's eyes embarrassed him. They were dry, direct, piercing, without emotion.

She spoke calmly, with careful spacing as if breath had to be apportioned for each word. "These policemen have not done anything. They said they had to wait for you. My son is dead. My only son. My only child. What are you going to do?"

"Why—" Damon stammered, "I know how you feel, Mrs. Pomfret—"

"You do not know how I feel." She closed her mouth, and her jaw twitched. She turned and gestured with her hand. "These people were in my house, invited here, and one of them killed my son." She leveled her eyes at Adolph Koch. "You." At Hebe Heath. "You." At Garda Tusar. "You." At Felix Beck...

Damon moved in front of her. "See here, Mrs. Pomfret," he said bluntly, "you ask what I'm going to do. First I'm going to find out what happened and how it happened. I can't just snap my fingers and truth jumps out of a box. All I know now is that your son drank something and died. This will be—"

"He cried out." Mrs. Pomfret's jaw twitched again, "He called to me. He started to come to me, with his face—he staggered and fell down and got up on his knees and fell again—"

She stopped.

"I can get this from someone else," Damon offered "I don't want— "

"No. I prefer to tell you myself. We were all in there except my husband and that man." She pointed: "Tecumseh Fox." She pointed again: "That is my husband." Again: "That is Dora Mowbray." She completed the roster, pronouncing the names clearly and precisely, excepting four men in uniform—two policemen and two servants. "We had all been in this room, and left my husband and Mr. Fox here and went to the yellow room. That is in front, the other side of the reception hall—"

"I just came from there."

"Then you—you've seen him—"

"Yes, I saw him. You understand, Mrs. Pomfret, it will be necessary—the body must be taken for an examination—"

"Taken? Away from here?"

"Yes. I have given the order—"

"I don't want that!"

"Naturally you don't. But you asked me what I'm going to do, and that's one of the things we do, and it's going to be done. However painful—Now here! Mrs. Pomfret!"

She was marching for the door. One of the two detectives who had entered with Damon was there, backed against the knob; she gestured him away, but he stood fast. The inspector was speaking:

"You can't go in there, Mrs. Pomfret!"

She turned, and he saw her eyes again. "I intend," she said, "to be present when my son's body is taken away."

Damon gave up. "All right," he said to the man at the door, "go along with her and tell Craig." The man nodded and opened the door. When it had closed behind them Damon turned and surveyed the field. Even disregarding the two policemen, the detective, and the two servants, there were so many of them....He frowned at Tecumseh Fox and inquired:

"So you weren't there when it happened?"

Fox, seated at a corner of the table, shook his head. "I was in here with Mr. Pomfret. When I got there Dunham was dead."

The inspector's eyes moved to a young man standing the other side of Fox's chair with his hands thrust into his pockets. "Your name is Theodore Gill?"

Ted nodded. "That's right."

"Where were you?"

Ted wet his lips and swallowed. "I was in there. Drinking a highball and talking with Miss Mowbray and Mr. Beck."

"Where was Dunham?"

"I don't know. I mean I didn't notice. He had been talking with his mother, but I suppose he had left to pour himself a drink. The first I knew, when he made a choking noise and cried out, he was in the alcove where the drinks were. He tottered a few steps and collapsed, and struggled to his knees and went down again—just as Mrs. Pomfret said. The first one to get to him was Mr. Zorilla."

"I was already there." Diego Zorilla's bass came from the other side of the room, and Damon turned to look at him. "I was getting Scotch and sodas for Miss Heath and myself when Perry came and poured his drink. I was right there when he poured it and drank it."

"Did he take it from the same bottle that you got yours from?"

"No, mine was Scotch. He always drank bourbon."

"Did he use the same soda bottle that you used?"

"He didn't use any. Drank it straight, right down. He often did that, with water for a chaser."

"Was Miss Heath in the alcove with you?"

"Not at that moment. I had gone to get a drink for myself, and she was there starting to mix one, and I offered to do it, and she went to a chair and sat down."

"What were you doing at the moment Dunham swallowed his drink?"

"I had picked up the two glasses and was putting them down again to close a window. Someone had opened a window in the alcove and the curtain was blowing, and Mrs. Pomfret called to me to close it. I never got it closed. While I was putting the glasses down I saw a peculiar look on Perry's face just as he gulped his drink—or just after—and he made a sort of a strangled noise. It didn't seem more than three seconds before he cried out and his face twisted up and he went into a stagger. If that drink did it, it was incredible how swift it was—"

"Why do you say 'If that drink did it?' Had he had one before that?"

Diego shook his head. "Not that I know of. I'm pretty sure he hadn't. He had been talking with his mother, at the divan at the end of the room."

"Then the glass he poured his drink into was clean? Not previously used?"

"I don't know. I suppose so. There was an assortment of them there on the traveling bar."

"And you were already there making Scotch and soda when he came up to pour his drink?"

"Yes."

"Right there facing him, watching him?"

"Watching him? Why would I be watching him?"

"Well, you were right there. If he had put anything in his drink from a vial or a box or an envelope, you would have seen him. Wouldn't you?"

"Yes, I would." Diego's eyes flickered and his lips twisted wryly. "And God knows I'd like to say I did. But I didn't."

"Why would you like to say you did?"

"I should think that's obvious. Though I wasn't especially fond of Perry Dunham, I wouldn't have regarded his suicide as a pleasant thing to happen. But it would have been a lot pleasanter than what seems to have happened." Diego slowly looked around. "One of us. Including me." He met the inspector's gaze. "I wasn't 'watching' him, as you put it. But unless he used sleight of hand, he didn't put anything in his glass except what he poured from the bottle."

"And that was from the bottle of bourbon there on the bar?"

"Yes."

Damon turned to the two menservants, standing side by side at the far wall. "Did either of you men take that bar in there?"

One of them spoke. "Yes, sir, I did." He appeared startled at the loudness of his own voice, and repeated four tones down, "I did, sir."

"What's your name?"

"Schaeffer, sir."

"When did you take it in?"

"When Mrs. Pomfret told me to. She rang—"

"Were these people already there?"

"Yes, sir." The man darted a glance around. "That is, most of them were."

"And you wheeled the bar in with the bottles and glasses already on it?"

"Yes, sir, and the ice, the bitters—"

"Including the bourbon?"

"Yes, sir. There is always Blue Grass bourbon, because that is the only kind Mr. Dunham will drink. I beg your pardon."

"What for?"

"I mean, the only kind Mr. Dunham did drink."

"Oh. How much was in the bourbon bottle? Do you know?"

"Yes, sir." Schaeffer allowed himself to look pleased. "I have been considering that point. I have expected to be asked that. The Blue Grass bourbon bottle was slightly less than half full."

"How do you know? Did you drink some?"

"No, sir. On serving the bar, if any bottle is less than half full, a full one is added. But I remember deciding that the bourbon would do, since no one drank it but Mr. Dunham."

"How did you know no one else would drink it?"

"It was known, sir. To the household. To everyone. That

Mr. Dunham drank nothing else. Most people take Scotch or rye or Irish. You would call it a deduction, sir."

"I would like hell." The inspector flushed. One of his weaknesses was that he never got along with trained menservants. He turned back to Diego Zorilla. "Did you drink any of that bourbon?"

Diego shook his head. "As I said, I drank Scotch."

"Any of you?" Damon looked around. "Did any of you drink bourbon? You, Mr. Koch?"

"No." Adolph Koch was seated across the room by the big screen, near Garda Tusar. Apparently there was an obstruction in his throat, and he cleared it out. "I had gin and bitters."

"Did you go to the bar and get it yourself?"

"Yes."

"You, Miss Tusar? What did you drink?"

"Vermouth cassis," Garda said promptly and clearly. "I went to the bar with Mr. Koch and he poured it for me."

"Miss Mowbray?"

"I had a glass of sherry." Dora's voice squeaked and she too had to clear her throat. "I poured one for myself and one for Mrs. Pomfret and took it to her."

"Mr. Beck?"

"I do not drink!" Beck declared explosively. He was seated in a chair backed up against the table, rubbing his knees with his palms. "I went to that—bar if you call it that—and poured a glass of water and put lemon juice in it and drank it!"

"Mr. Gill. What was in your highball?"

"Rye," Ted said succinctly.

"And Miss Heath, Mr. Zorilla says he took you Scotch and soda. You drank no bourbon?"

Hebe didn't get to answer. Felix Beck's voice, with a ring of accusation in it, forestalled her:

"Certainly she didn't! She knew better! She picked the bottle up and threw it out of the window!"

# 8

HEBE HEATH clutched her breasts and tilted her chin to stare blue-eyed defiance up at the inspector. Adolph Koch half rose from his chair, muttering something, and sank back again. Ted Gill stepped across, put his hand on the back of Hebe's chair, stood there as a protector, and sighed heavily. Damon's gaze slanted down to the brave glory of Hebe's matchless eyes, and then he took a step toward her and inquired:

"Well?"

"Well," she whispered.

"Did you throw that bottle out of the window?"

She nodded.

"You did?"

She nodded.

"Why?"

Her hands abandoned their clutch on her breasts and flew straight for the inspector in appeal, to the length of her outstretched arms. "Oh," she cried softly, "it was an ungovernment impulse!"

Tecumseh Fox stirred in his seat and looked away from her. The others stared at her in soundless fascination, then transferred to Henry Pomfret when a noise came from him—a spasmodic tremoloso titter. He looked around abashed, and said pugnaciously to no one, "I'm sorry," and caught his lip with his teeth. Ted Gill spoke at Damon in a patient and determined voice:

"She means ungovernable. Miss Heath is sensitive and high-strung. She is emotionally unstable. She is impetuous, mercurial, galvanic. She is an artist—"

"I'm not asking her for a character analysis," said Damon.

"Or you either, Mr. Gill. I'm asking her why she threw that bottle out of the window."

"And I'm telling you. You are dealing with an extraordinary person. She becomes seized with an irresistible desire to do something, and she does it. It's a kind of trance. Then it goes out of her mind. She does not now actually remember picking up that bottle and throwing it—"

Damon snorted. "She just admitted it!"

"She admitted it because three of us saw her do it and have—mentioned it to her. Miss Mowbray, Mr. Beck, and myself. At the moment she did it, Mrs. Pomfret was kneeling beside her son, Koch and Miss Tusar were bending over her, and Zorilla had gone after Fox. I was standing with Miss Mowbray and I said the bottle he drank out of ought to be corked but I didn't know which one, and she said he always drank bourbon. I reached for it, but Miss Heath grabbed it and made one of her—made a gesture, a dramatic gesture, and hurled it out of the window. When Fox came I told him, and I also told the first policeman who appeared. But I knew by the look on her face, a kind of, uh, exaltation, that she didn't know what she was doimg—"

"Bah!" Felix Beck was out of his chair, trembling with indignation. "Her an artist! Not know what she was doing? Hah! She's a Circe! An evil witch! First Jan, I warned him about her, and now this—"

"Oh, can it!" Ted snapped at him. "It's bad enough without a lot of yapping—"

"Both of you can it," Damon commanded sharply. He confronted Hebe. "I'll talk with you later, Miss Heath, but I'll ask you now, is Mr. Gill correct? Do you do things and forget about them?"

"Oh," she breathed.

"Well, do you?"

"I don't know." Her lovely hands were clasped tight and pulled against her shape. "Oh, I don't know!"

"Do you become seized with an irresistible desire to do something, and do it? Did you become seized with such a desire to put something into that bottle of bourbon?"

"To put ..." She goggled at him. Her hands unclasped, and tension left the muscles of her face. "Put something *in* the bottle?" she demanded incredulously, in an entirely new tone. "Don't be a damn fool!"

Damon grunted, and regarded her in silence. He raised a hand to scratch the back of his neck, and still gazed at her.

"May I suggest—" Tecumseh Fox began.

"No," Damon said shortly. His eyes swept an arc around the faces, around to the left, slowly, and back to the right. "It is my duty to inform you," he said in a tone of displeasure, "that there is a presumption that Perry Dunham was murdered. I'll have to talk with each of you separately before you're allowed to leave here, and that will take a long time. May I have a room to use, Mr. Pomfret?"

"Certainly. My wife..." Pomfret hesitated. "But of course. Or we'll go somewhere else and you can use this."

"That will do fine. You and your wife will go where you please. In your house. But the rest of you will stay together in one room, with law officers present. I have the right to enforce that under the circumstances, but I would appreciate it if you will co-operate. I ask you to consider the possibility that the murderer of Perry Dunham is among you. If you don't like that idea, neither do I. Now one thing. If there was poison in that bourbon, it could have been put there at any time since somebody last drank from it. It wasn't necessarily put there in that room this afternoon. But it might have been. If it was, the container that held the poison is probably somewhere around, unless it was thrown out of the window the way the bottle was. That room is being searched, and the whole house will be. Each of you will be questioned about your movements. But there is a chance that the container is concealed on the person of someone. I think it would be a good plan if you would all allow yourselves to be searched. I think you should agree to that. For the ladies, I can have a policewoman here in five minutes."

They shrank. They glanced at each other, and back at the inspector, and away. If the murderer was there, he had no reason to fear exposing himself by a unique reluctance,

for reluctance and distaste were on all faces except that of
Tecumseh Fox. He nodded at Damon:

"Good here. That's sensible. Though probably futile."

"It is an indignity," Felix Beck growled.

Hebe said, "It's horribly revolting."

The door opened, and eyes went to it. A man entered
and spoke across the room to Damon: "Craig wants you,
Inspector," and Damon nodded and tramped out. Everybody decided all at once that their muscles were cramped
and shifted to new positions in their chairs or on their
feet. Low-voiced mutterings started. Adolph Koch asked
Fox if they could be legally compelled to submit to a
search, and Fox said no, and Ted Gill said they might as
well submit anyway. Beck folded his arms and paced up
and down, and a policeman yawned. Schaeffer, who had
served the bar, expounded something lengthily to his
colleague in an undertone. Tecumseh Fox leaned far backwards and stared at the ceiling, and was still in that
position five minutes later when the door opened again
and the inspector entered. He walked across to the end of
the big table, which was about the geographical center of
the assemblage, and held up an object in his hand for all to
see.

"Do any of you recognize this?"

"Certainly." Henry Pomfret spoke up. "It's my Ju Chou
incense bowl. Please don't drop it!"

"I won't." Damon's big hand had an adequate grip on
the beautiful little bowl of red and misty pearly green.
"How long has it been kept on that stand in that room?"

"A long time. A couple of years."

"Is it used to drop things into? Like an ash tray?"

"Not if I know it, it isn't. Sometimes some ass drops a
cigarette in it."

"Well, this time it wasn't a cigarette." There was a note
of grim satisfaction in the inspector's voice. He put the
bowl down on the table, and took from it, with his thumb
and forefinger, a ball of crumpled paper; and displayed it
as a prestidigitator displays a coin he has plucked from the
air. "It was this. I'm not going to open it out. One of my
men did, part way. It's a piece of ordinary bond paper, and

clinging to it are particles of white powder. He dampened a little of it, and it smells like cyanide. So I withdraw my request that you permit yourselves to be searched."

There was a stir, a rustle, and dead silence. It was broken by Henry Pomfret.

"Christ," he muttered incredulously. "In the incense bowl. Then ..."

"Then what, Mr. Pomfret?"

"Nothing." Pomfret shook his head as in disbelief. "Nothing."

"Did the fact that this was found in the bowl suggest something to you?"

"No! Nothing!"

Damon gazed at him and persisted. "Did it perhaps remind you that you saw someone go to that bowl and drop something in it?"

"No! It didn't remind me of anything! I was merely going to say that this makes it—that someone here did it. If I had seen anyone drop something in that bowl I'd have fished it out; I always do. Anyway, I wasn't there, I was in here with Fox."

"But you might," Fox put it, "have seen it earlier in the afternoon." He looked at the inspector. "I was going to suggest before that you may have got a wrong impression from what Schaeffer said. He told you that he served the bar when Mrs. Pomfret rang and told him to. When these people—most of them, he said—were already there. But that wasn't when they left Pomfret and me here and went to the yellow room, it was before we came to this room at all. I arrived at a quarter past two and the bar was in there then, and everyone else was present." He returned to Pomfret. "So you could have seen someone drop something into the bowl then, couldn't you?"

"I suppose I could," Pomfret admitted gruffly. "But I didn't."

"I did," said a voice.

Swift glances darted to Garda Tusar.

"Who?" Damon barked.

Garda, ignoring him, left her chair over by the big screen, near Adolph Koch, and came around the end of the table. She intended, apparently, to face someone, and she did. It was Dora Mowbray. Garda's black eyes blazed down, and Dora's came up to meet them.

"You did it," Garda said. "I saw you. You went over to the stand—"

There was simultaneous and universal movement; it was as if the nervous systems of those well-behaved people had been adjusted to absorb so much strain and no more. Felix Beck snarled, Hebe gasped, Diego arose so precipitately that he overturned his chair...but the chief performers were Ted Gill and Henry Pomfret. Ted sprang through space, seized Garda's arm and violently whirled her around; she lost her balance, toppled against the table, and knocked the incense bowl off onto the floor; Pomfret yelled and leaped, grabbed for the bowl and missed, spun around, doubled his fist and crashed it against Ted's jaw; the detective and policemen, rushing up, got their hands on Pomfret, on Ted, on Garda—

"Back off!" Damon commanded sharply. He glared at Pomfret. "What the hell was that for?"

"I'm sorry," Pomfret said, but didn't sound sorry. He was panting. He stooped to get the bowl, which was intact.

Ted's eyes were glittering at Garda. "I would like," he said through his teeth, "to pass that tap on to you with interest. I don't know why you've got it in for Miss Mowbray, but you try any more of that raving—"

"Ted!" Dora was there, with a hand on his arm. "Please! She wasn't raving. I did drop that paper into the bowl."

Ted gawked at her. The inspector whirled:

"You did?"

"Yes."

There was a stunned silence.

"By God," Diego growled. "My little Dora—"

"No, Diego." Dora shook her head at him. "Your little Dora didn't put poison in Perry's whisky." Her lip trembled, then it curled in sudden anger and her face flared. "Look at you! All of you! Your faces! You believe—just because I—Oh, if my father was here! Everything has been hateful—ever since he died—"

"I'm here!" Ted sang at her.

Damon gazing at her, said dryly, "About dropping that paper in the bowl."

"I did." Dora's eyes met his. "I said I did. It was in my bag."

"Who put it there?"

"I don't know. I found it there when we were leaving the yellow room to come in here." She picked up a brown cloth handbag from her chair, held it up, and indicated an outside compartment made with an extra fold of the cloth. "It was in here. I saw the bulge and stuck my fingers in to see what it was. I had no idea where it came from. It looked like nothing but a crumpled piece of paper, and I dropped it in the bowl as I went by."

"You are saying that someone put it in there while the bag was in your possession."

"I am not. I didn't say that. I left the bag lying on a sofa in the yellow room when Perry—when I went to the other end of the room with Mr. Dunham."

"And it was when you got it again that you noticed the bulge in it?"

"Yes."

"How long was the bag lying on the sofa?"

"Well, it was—fifteen or twenty minutes."

"Why did you go to the other end of the room with Dunham?"

"Because he said he wanted to speak to me."

"What about?"

"About—something—a personal matter."

"Were you engaged to marry Dunham?"

"That's none of your business. But I wasn't."

The inspector grunted. "You'll probably be surprised," he said crustily, "at what the police regard as their business in a murder investigation. And what we don't get one way we get another. If we can. Were you in love with Dunham?"

"Good heavens, no!"

"Did you hate him?"

"No."

"Were you an intimate friend of his?"

"No." Dora frowned. "I have known him all my life. His mother and my father were friends."

"I'd like to know what it was he wanted to speak to you about this afternoon. If you refuse to tell me, you can't blame me if I—"

"I don't refuse to tell you. He wanted to know about the other note Jan left. Whether I had seen it—whether I had read any of it."

"Note? Who is Jan?"

"Jan Tusar," Tecumseh Fox broke in. "He committed suicide—shot himself—last Monday evening at Carnegie Hall. I think you're going to have to shuffle that into your deck, and I can save you a lot of time on it." His eyes took in the others. "You folks understand, of course, that there is no longer any question of going to the police with the violin business. The police are here. I suggest, Inspector, if you want to cut some corners, that you get together with me and a man with a notebook....By the way, Miss Tusar, since the police are here, how about that thing you were saving for them? You might as well hand it over now. You can't do any better than the chief of the Homicide Squad."

Garda, who had dropped into a chair beside Diego, opened her handbag and took out the envelope and held it out to Damon. He glanced at the address and then removed the enclosure and looked at it:

THOSE WHO SEEK TO DAMAGE THE REICH WILL SUFFER FOR IT AS YOUR BROTHER DID. HEIL HITLER!

"My God," he muttered in disgust, "one of those things." He regarded Garda in bewilderment. "Then you were married to Tusar? And Dunham was your brother?"

Garda stared at him.

"No," Fox said impatiently, "the violinist was her brother. That's one small item of the background, which I'm offering you at a bargain. Unless you prefer to slash your way through the brush—"

"Thanks, I'll take it. I like bargains." Damon addressed the group: "A while ago I asked you folks to co-operate by staying together in one room. Now, in view of finding that paper in that bowl, as well as other things, I instruct you to do so. I'm going to start with Fox, and you'll be notified when I'm ready for you. Ryder, take a man and stay with them. Mr. Pomfret, will you kindly lead the way to a room where they can sit down? And Ryder, send Kossoy in with a notebook, and tell Craig I want to see him."

## 9

"I WOULDN'T call it a bargain at any price," Inspector Damon declared in a tone of complete disrelish. "It looks to me like the worst damn mess I ever saw in my life."

He was seated at an end of the big table, with Fox at his right and Detective Kossoy, his brow puckered in concentration at his notebook, at his left. They had been there nearly an hour. There had been a few interruptions— among them a phone call from the laboratory to say that a high percentage of potassium cyanide had been found in the whisky in the medicine dropper which had been retrieved from the dent in the top of the sedan, and one from the assistant medical examiner also reporting cyanide—but mostly Fox had talked. It was all down in Kossoy's notebook, all that Fox had seen and heard; he had even relinquished to the inspector an envelope containing the morsel of varnish he had scraped from the violin.

Fox got up and stretched his legs, sat down again, and said, "It may be a mess, but still you got a bargain. People have paid good money for a report like that."

Damon nodded. He looked at Fox obliquely. "One thing you haven't mentioned. Where do you come in?"

"I'm not in. Not professionally." Fox smiled at the morose eyes and prizefighter's jaw. "Really, you can cross me off. I haven't held out a thing. That is, no facts. Of course I may have made a few deductions, as Schaeffer would call them...."

"Yeah. Why the hell don't a big strong man like that get a job? What kind of deductions, for instance?"

"Deductions come much higher than reports."

"I thought you said you weren't in this. What do you want?"

"Nothing. Frankly, Inspector, you're perfectly welcome to this case, including the murder—if not legally murder, still murder—of Jan Tusar. Don't forget that item, because it's a part of your problem. I was having a try at it, but it felt dead in my hands. I was leery of it. It was too slick and too subtle. To kill a man by spilling varnish into a violin! Can you construe the mind that thought of that? I hope you can. You'll have to, if you're going to get the murderer of Perry Dunham."

"You think the two are connected. You think Dunham knew something about the varnish in the violin, and you let the cat loose when you told about him going for the violin when he thought you had gone, and that's why he was killed." Damon grunted. "You may be right, but if that's one of the deductions you're holding for a rise in the market—"

"Oh, that's nothing to brag about," Fox conceded. "But here's a nice little trick." He got a memo pad from his pocket and uncapped his pen. "Look here." With the others leaning over to watch, he made two drawings on the pad:

"Quite a trick," Damon said sarcastically. "Do you think you could learn to do it, Kossoy?"

Fox, ignoring him, requested, "Let me have that thing Miss Tusar gave you." He took the envelope Damon handed him, removed the sheet of paper, and put it on the table beside the pad. "Now. Which one of my swastikas is like the one on the note from the Nazi? You see the difference, of course."

"Certainly. The one on the left."

"Correct. And that's the traditional design of the swastika, the design that the Chinese have used for centuries as a good luck symbol. But when Hitler took it for a trademark, he either made a mistake or deliberately switched it—anyhow, the Nazi swastika is like the one on the right. No Nazi would ever make one like the one on the left. So it wasn't a Nazi that sent that thing to Miss Tusar. It's a phony."

"I'm a son of a gun," Kossoy muttered. "Can I have that?"

Fox tore the sheet from the pad and handed it to him, and put the note in the envelope and returned it to Damon. "That," he remarked, "will help a little. At least you won't have to waste time trying to connect one of them with Berlin or the Bund. I only hope it's not the only mistake the weasel made. If it is, you're more than welcome."

Damon was frowning at him. "You heard me tell my office to put twenty men on a check up and give special attention to the Nazi angle."

"I did," Fox admitted, "and it made me envious. An army like that ready to go!"

"Have you got any more nice little tricks?"

"Well..." Fox considered. "They go over better when they're spaced out. Of course you're going to get a pack of lies, as usual, but in my opinion you'll get none from Miss Mowbray. She would lie in an emergency—naturally, anybody would—but I doubt if she has anything to lie about, and I believe her story about the paper that had the poison in it. Diego Zorilla is a friend of mine. That doesn't convince you that he didn't poison Dunham, but it does me—till further notice. You can have the rest of them except Mrs. Pomfret, I suppose, but even that carries no written guarantee."

"I know the multiplication tables myself. I mean tricks."

Fox shook his head. "The bag's empty. If I were going to work on this, which I'm not, thank God, I'd have to start on a blank page." He returned the pad and pen to his pockets, pushed back his chair, and arose.

"Where you going?"

"That depends. If you'll give me a passport I'll go home. If not, I suppose I'll have to join—"

The inspector snorted in disbelief. "Sure you'd like to go home. And leave this hanging here? Not if I know you. And I do know you. If I send you in there with the crowd—you stay here. Sit down. There by Kossoy."

Fox smiled at him. "I'm not making any contract. In case I do happen to think of a trick."

"Neither am I." Damon turned to a man in uniform who was seated by the door: "Ask Mrs. Pomfret to come here."

It was a few minutes short of seven o'clock when Mrs. Pomfret entered the library. It was after midnight when the cook's assistant, the last of the procession, left. When the door had closed behind him, Inspector Damon muttered in weary legato a string of the most impressive and pungent terms of profanity, and, his eyes bloodshot with strain, glared with savage repugnance at the two notebooks in front of Detective Kossoy which were filled with scratches from cover to cover.

"Anyway," Fox sighed, "the smoked turkey sandwiches were good."

"One of those people," Damon growled, "poisoned that man."

Which certainly was not much of a show for six hours' hard work, but that was as far as they had got. No one had been able to furnish a conjecture regarding a breast that might have harbored a desire to kill Perry Dunham. Many of them had confessed to various degrees of dislike for him. Though it was now established that the poison had been put in the whisky, not after their return from the library but during their preliminary assemblage in the yellow room, it had not been possible to eliminate anyone from the list; no one was positive that any other one had not gone near the bar. On the other hand, no one had admitted observing any suspicious action by anyone else—any handling of the bourbon bottle, or prolonged lingering at the bar, or telltale tension or agitation. In sum, if anyone had seen anything which might have guided ever so slightly the finger of accusation, he had not disclosed it. Even Garda admitted that there had been nothing furtive or wary about Dora's movements when she dropped the ball of paper into the bowl; she had merely, openly, gone to the stand and tossed it in.

Three of them—Koch, Dora, and Henry Pomfret—were sure that Perry had not had a drink before they left the yellow room for the library, and that left wide open the question of when the bourbon had been poisoned. It was not even positive, though of course highly probable, that it had been done in the yellow room. The servants stated that the bourbon had been kept, along with other liquors, in an unlocked cupboard in the pantry; and Schaeffer said that he had outfitted the bar there and wheeled it directly to the yellow room. The question of when a drink had last been poured from the bourbon bottle was also open; no one knew with certainty.

The one known and admitted action that would normally have been at least a starting point for a trail had apparently been an incredible and fantastic bizarrerie; by the time it came Hebe's turn in the library, all memory of throwing the bottle from the window had passed from her mind. That's what she said. Her session had ended with Damon staring speechless into her glorious eyes, and Fox had mercifully intervened and instructed the policeman to take her out.

The police commissioner had come, stayed an hour, and departed. The district attorney had arrived around nine o'clock and left at midnight. Fuller reports had been received from the laboratory and the morgue; Sergeant Craig and his squad of experts had finished and gone; the gaping jaws of the press had been given bones to close on; men had been sent with a key to Perry's bachelor apartment on 51st Street to examine his papers and belongings for a possible hint; the police captain who had investigated Tusar's suicide had been hustled out of bed for a visit to the district attorney's office.

Still the most that could be said was what Inspector Damon growled from a tired throat at 12:40 A.M., "One of those people poisoned that man."

Fox abandoned his chair and jerked himself into shape. "Well," he declared, "if you still think I wouldn't like to go home, try me. As a matter of fact, I'm ready to give an imitation of an indignant citizen. Would you care to see it?"

Damon shook his head, rubbed his eyes with his fingers, blinked at the incense bowl to recover a focus, and stood up. "Okay," he said disgustedly. "Bring your notebooks, Kossoy, I guess there's nothing else in here we want." He started for the door, speaking to the man in uniform: "Show me where they are."

Fox followed them, down the corridor and across the reception hall into the vast chamber which Pomfret had called the cathedral. It might, on that occasion, have been better called a mausoleum, or an even more dismal term if there is one. Even the two policemen on guard, one at each end of the room, seemed to have succumbed to the pervasive miasma of gloom. Seven haggard faces—for the Pomfrets were not there—turned to the entrance as the inspector appeared; Koch from a chair near one occupied by Hebe Heath, Diego from a window at the far side where he stood with Felix Beck, Dora from a divan on which she was stretched out, Ted Gill from under a lamp where he sat with a newspaper, Garda from a seat near one of the pianos. Koch started to blurt something, but Damon raised a hand:

"We're leaving here," he announced curtly. "You folks can go. I may need one or all of you again in the morning, and I'll expect you to be available at the addresses you have given. None of you is to leave the city. If you ladies would like to be escorted home..."

Ted's newspaper had dropped to the floor and he was on

his feet. "I'll take Miss Mowbray," he said aggressively, striding to the divan. "If I may?"

She was sitting up. She protested feebly, "It isn't necessary. . . ."

"And me?" Hebe Heath inquired tragically. Disheveled and forlorn, she was more ravishing than ever. "Oh, Ted!"

"If you'll allow me the pleasure, Miss Heath." Adolph Koch was bowing to her with admirable social grace, under the circumstances.

"You, Miss Tusar?" Damon asked.

"I'll take her," Diego Zorilla offered gruffly, with no social grace whatever.

"No, you won't," Garda declared. Blear though her eyes were, they still could flash. "I'll take a taxi...."

Diego shrugged and turned to Fox. "Are you going? For God's sake, let's get out of here." He headed for the arch.

Fox followed him. In the reception hall a manservant got their things for them while a plain-clothes man looked on. They had to wait a moment for word from Damon to pass them. The elevator man abandoned all decorum and discipline and stared at them all the way down. The night lobby staff also stared, as did the members of a little group under the canopy on the sidewalk: the doorman, two policemen, and two or three young fellows, one of whom pounced on Fox.

"Listen, Mr. Fox, I've been waiting for you, this is a natural for two columns with a by-line..."

It took a block of brisk walking and brisk words to shake him off.

"My gloves are in my right pocket," Diego grumbled. "I always put them in the left."

"Sure," Fox nodded, "they went through everything. My car's around the corner in Sixty-ninth. Can I give you a lift?"

"I want a drink."

"You've had nothing to do but drink for the past seven hours."

"I couldn't, not there. I swallowed a little Scotch and

damn near threw it up. My stomach isn't settled yet. How about coming down to my place for a sandwich?"

"I can tell you what you want to know in one sentence. The police have no more idea who killed Dunham than you have."

But Diego protested that he wanted more than that, he wanted the company of his friend with a sandwich and a drink, and though Fox objected that he had sixty miles to drive and needed eight hours sleep and intended to prune grape vines in the morning, he consented. They drove in his car, stopping at an all-night delicatessen on the way to get sandwiches, to Diego's address on 54th Street, an old brownstone house, and mounted two flights of stairs to his apartment. Even with its polygenetic and rather shabby furnishings, the medium-sized living room was comfortable and not unattractive, and Diego did the honors with a Spanish flourish, taking Fox's hat and coat and disposing of them in the closet.

"I'll serve the feast," he proposed. "Soda with yours?"

"I don't suppose I could have coffee?"

"Sure. I make mine for breakfast. Ten minutes."

"That'll be marvelous. You'd make some woman a good wife. I want to wash my hands."

"That door over there."

Fox went to the bathroom. Behind the closed door he permitted himself the luxury of a wanton yawn, succeeded by a scowl of dissatisfaction. He did intend to prune grape vines in the morning, but when he did that kind of work he liked to enjoy it, to taste it, and he knew his mind too well to suppose that under the present circumstances it would be content to devote itself to the questions of spurs and fruiting canes. Even now, when he was sleepy or should be, only by a sustained effort of the will could he prevent it from diving into the fascinating problem of the cerebral processes of Hebe Heath....

He got his hands washed with soap, and his face doused, and looked for a towel. There was none on the rack, nor on the hook on the door. At the left was a smaller door, and he opened it, disclosing shelves with towels aplenty as well as a miscellany of other objects. He took a turkish, preferring them always to smooth ones, got his face dried, and, as he wiped his hands, ran his eyes over the array of articles on the shelves. But in spite of that display of idle curiosity, and of his trained capacity of observation, he would not have seen it but for his remarkably sharp vision, for the closet was dim. As it was, he did see it, the upper side of it, behind a pile of washcloths, peered in at it, and finally reached in and brought it to the light.

Under the light he examined it with a gathering frown. The pure black glaze. The delicate decorations in white enamel at the bottom. The golden yellow dragons and flowers in the middle, interspersed with the feathery green twigs and leaves. The odd, even unique, shape—Pomfret had said "unique."

There could be no doubt about it. It was Pomfret's Wan Li black rectangular, a picture of which he had shown to Fox, and which Mrs. Pomfret was convinced had been stolen by Hebe Heath.

# 10

FOX PUT the vase back in the closet, shut the door, turned to the basin, and began to wash his hands again. A little consideration was required to decide how to handle it. He was, of course, under no compulsion to handle it at all; however the thing had got to Diego's closet, it had nothing to do with pruning grape vines. But it was ridiculous to expect any animal with a monkey for an ancestor not to meddle with a thing like that. Fox used the towel on his hands, got the vase from the closet, opened the door and stepped into the living room, and called:

"Hey, Diego, where did you get this?"

"What?" Diego stuck his head out of the kitchenette the

other side of the room. "Where did I get what? Oh—"

He saw it. His face stiffened. He was motionless a
moment, then started across.

"It's a peach," Fox said enthusiastically. "Where did you
get it?

"That thing?" Diego growled. "Why—I don't know.
Somebody gave it to me." He started to put out a hand for
it, then let the hand drop. "Why, is it any good?"

"It certainly is. I'm not an expert, but I think it's a
sixteenth-century Ming. What'll you take for it?"

"Oh, I—How did you happen to see it? Looking for an
aspirin?"

"No, a towel. There wasn't any on the rack. Really, I'd
like to buy it."

"Sure you would." Diego laughed, not too successfully.
"I never saw anything yet you wouldn't like to buy. But
I—uh—that is, I'd hate to stick you. I doubt if it's worth
much of anything—don't see how it can be. How did you
happen to see it—it's dark in there...."

"I'm cat-eyed. Caught a glimpse of the green and gold
enamel." Fox put the vase down on a table. "Let me know
if you decide to sell it. I smell coffee, don't I?"

When, half an hour later, Fox departed, no further
reference had been made to the vase. It was of course
natural, in view of the events of the day, that the comradely
consumption of sandwiches and coffee should not have
assumed the character of a festivity, but Diego had been so
sour and glum that it might reasonably have been asked
why he had requested the company of his friend at all.

So Fox, driving home through a ghostly and swirling
night mist that kept him down to forty miles an hour, had
still another puzzlement to harass him. It was as good as
certain that Diego knew that the vase in his bathroom
closet was the stolen property of Henry Pomfret, had been
the most highly prized treasure of the Pomfret collection.
It was next to certain that Diego had not stolen it, or if he
had, that it had been for a more complicated and romantic motive than the acquisition of an article of value. No, it
was impossible to fit Diego, as known, into the frame of so
commonplace a vulgarity....

For a solid week that enigma, and others more or less persistent, kept dodging nimbly around in Fox's brain, trying to keep out of his way. For seven days he pruned vines and trees, started hot-beds and cold frames, removed top layers of winter mulch, repaired fences, helped a cow have a calf, and performed a hundred chores which ordinarily he left to Sam Trimble and those of the Zoo's guests who felt like making a token payment for their board and room. It was his annual salute to the approaching spring. There was one interruption, on Tuesday, when a phone call from New York requested his presence at the district attorney's office, which resulted in no enlightenment on either side; and of evenings he read the newspapers. But in spite of the dozens of columns throughout the week on the subject of the Dunham murder and its link to the spectacular suicide of Jan Tusar, all of the enigmas remained intact. Still they made it readable and even exciting. The press had somehow got onto the varnish in the violin, whether or not by official communiqué was not made clear, and of course that was honey. The *Gazette* even printed a picture of the violin itself, so stated, with a daggerlike arrow pointing to the f-hole through which the varnish had been poured, which was an extraordinary journalistic achievement, considering that the violin was still in the vault at the Day and Night Bank where Fox had put it.

Wednesday a sideshow got the black headlines—a divagation conceived, planned and executed by Hebe Heath. It had all the earmarks, Fox remarked as he read it, of her peculiar genius: simplicity, lightning abruptness, and spotless imbecility. She had taken an airplane for Mexico City, and, what was more, had got there; and, besought telegraphically, refused to return. Thursday she was still there, but Mr. Theodore Gill had gone after her. Friday they were both in Mexico City and not, apparently, preparing to travel. Saturday the *Gazette* gave the police the devil for letting Gill slip out of their clutches by a subterfuge; but in the Sunday morning papers he had brought her back.

She granted interviews. She had left New York to

escape publicity. (That, Fox decided, was her master-
piece.) She had had two good reasons for choosing Mexico
City: First, she had never been there before, and second,
the first long-distance plane to leave New York after her
decision to go was scheduled for there. She hadn't the
faintest desire to flee from an obligation to co-operate in
the processes of the law; to do that, she declared, would
be horribly revolting....Fox clipped the interview from
the *Times* and put it in his scrapbook.

Monday morning he got a telephone call from Mrs.
Pomfret. There was a drag to her voice that he had not
heard before; indeed, he would scarcely have recognized
it. She asked him to come to see her as soon as possible.
He said he would be there at two that afternoon.

He arrived punctually on the hour, and from a corner of
the reception hall was taken in a private elevator to the
second floor of the duplex apartment and along a corridor
to a chamber more feminine in its scents and silks than
anything he would have expected of her—a sitting room or
dressing room; the latter, he thought. The curtains were
drawn, but even in the half light he could see that her face
was as changed as her voice; the merry shrewd eyes were
glassy slits between red-rimmed lids, and the skin that
Rubens would have admired was leaden and lusterless.
That Fox saw as he crossed to where she sat and took the
hand she offered.

"I'm played out," she said—an explanation, not a bid for
sympathy. "I get dizzy if I stand up. Take that chair, it's the
most comfortable. You've just had a shave."

Fox smiled at her. "You should have seen me this
morning."

"I'm glad I didn't. I want you to find out who murdered
my son."

Fox screwed up his lips. "Well, Mrs. Pomfret—"

"Somebody has to. It has been a week. It has been eight
days. I don't want you to think I'm a vindictive old woman."

"I shouldn't suppose, right now, it matters much to you
what I think."

"Well, you're wrong. It does." She took a handkerchief
and dabbed at her eyes. "I'm not crying, it's just that my

eyes are sore. I've always disapproved of vindictive people, and I wouldn't want anyone to think that I'm one
myself. But you ought to be able to realize how it is. Right
here in my house, right in front of my eyes, my son died.
Murdered by one of those people. Is it reasonable to
expect me to drag along like this indefinitely, maybe
forever, not knowing who did it? Some of them were my
friends! I asked my lawyer to investigate you."

"That's all right. I've been investigated before."

"I suppose you have. He reported that you are flashy
but dependable and sound. I didn't want a slick shyster.
He also found an old rumor about your killing two men on
account of something about a young woman."

Fox froze. For a second he sat rigid and immobile, then
he stood up. "If what you want is rumors," he said icily,
and was going. An exclamation to his back did not stop
him; but before he reached the door fingers with a grip of
surprising strength closed on his arm, and he halted. She
was exigent but not apologetic:

"This is absurd! Did I know you were touchy about it? I
merely blurted it out! I do blurt things—"

"It's a bad habit, Mrs. Pomfret. Please let go of my
arm."

She relinquished her grip, let her hand fall, retreated a
step, and looked up at him, unflinching at the cold penetration of his eyes. "Don't go," she said. "I beg your
pardon. I suppose it is a bad habit. I need you. I form my
own judgments of people. I told my lawyer I intended to
engage you, and it was he who wanted to investigate you.
I didn't need to. When Diego told me of your contribution
to the fund for Jan's violin, naturally I thought you were
doing it to gain an entrée to my circle, but when you
declined my invitation to the presentation party, obviously
that wasn't it. But you're not going to decline this. I won't
let you. I don't care whether you think I'm a vindictive old
woman or not. The police have accomplished nothing.
Either they have no wits or they're outwitted."

She swayed a little, steadied herself. "I can't stand up for
two minutes. I can't sleep and I won't take things. This has
hit me—hit me cruelly—Give me your arm, please?"

Fox moved to her side and let her have his elbow for a support back to her chair. It was credible that she was in fact shattered—must have been, indeed, since she had twice applied the phrase "old woman" to herself, which would have been unthinkable ten days ago. Besides, it was always the case that if and when super-egotists finally get it, they get it good and hard.

"Sit down," she said. "If you wish, I'll beg your pardon again. I can't undertake to change my habits, not even now. Wait, before you sit down, get that check there under that vase on the table. As a retainer. If it isn't enough, say so."

"There's no hurry about that." Fox sat. "Are you sure you want to hire me for this job, Mrs. Pomfret?"

"Certainly I am. I don't do things unless I'm sure I want to. Why shouldn't I be?"

"Because, as you said, some of those people are your friends. You said 'were.' If I take the job I'll either finish it or break a leg. What if, for instance, Dora Mowbray did it?"

"Dora? She didn't."

"She could have. Or your husband, or Diego. I ask you to consider that seriously. This isn't a matter of a stolen vase or varnish in a violin; it's premeditated murder. If I, hired by you, get proof of guilt, it won't be reported privately and exclusively to you. One of those people will be tried and convicted and will die. That's all right with me. Is it all right with you?"

"Die," she said harshly. She repeated it, "Die...."

Fox nodded. "That's the penalty."

"My son died. In agony. I saw it. Didn't he?"

"He did."

"Then—yes."

"Very well. Please tell me what your son said to you Sunday afternoon. When I wanted to ask him about the violin and you insisted on speaking with him first."

Mrs. Pomfret blinked her red-rimmed eyes. "You were there when the inspector asked me that and I told him. He said nothing."

"I know. You said he laughed at you, reassured you, swore that in taking the violin from the parcel he had only been pulling my leg. But you're not talking to the police now, you're talking to your hired man, and believe me, your son's going for that violin was not for fun and games. There was nothing funny about it. I'd like to know exactly what he said when you asked him about it."

An hour later Fox was still there and Mrs. Pomfret was still on her chair, her shoulders sagging, answering his questions. Another hour later she was reclining on a chaise longue with her eyes closed and Fox was seated beside her, still asking. It was going on five o'clock when he finally left. He took with him a great many things he had not had on his arrival, among them the following:

### IN HIS POCKET, OBJECTS

A check for $5,000.

A key to Perry Dunham's bachelor apartment on 51st Street.

A note with the salutation, "To Whom It May Concern," signed by Mrs. Pomfret.

### IN HIS MEMORY, STATEMENTS BY MRS. POMFRET

She suspected that Perry had been carrying on an affair with Garda Tusar, from remarks Jan had made; but her recollection of the remarks was vague.

Garda had broken an engagement to marry Diego Zorilla when the accidental loss of his fingers had ruined his career, and Diego was still hopelessly infatuated with her.

The Wan Li vase had been stolen at the party given by her for presentation of the violin to Jan.

Hebe Heath should be in jail.

If Hebe had not stolen the vase, Adolph Koch had, for his own collection, which was "much inferior to my husband's."

Koch was a goat and a libertine.

### IN HIS MIND, CONCLUSIONS DRAWN

Mrs. Pomfret had had genuine affection for Perry and grieved for him, but it was the outrage to her ego—her son foully and impudently murdered before her eyes—that was intolerable and must be avenged.

Mrs. Pomfret's implacable hostility toward Hebe was the conventional wifely reaction of a woman as old as (older than?) her husband.

Mrs. Pomfret had wanted Perry to marry Dora Mowbray.

Most of which, Fox reflected as, reaching the sidewalk, he sought a drugstore for a phone booth, was not without interest as subsidiary material for a student of mankind, but it appeared to have little or no bearing on the questions of who poisoned Perry Dunham or drove Jan Tusar to suicide. Worse, the only line of inquiry it suggested was the one most distasteful to him personally; but he had taken the job.

He called the number of Diego's apartment, got no answer, tried the Metropolitan Broadcasting Company studios, and found him there. Diego was gruff and scarcely civil; he was busy with a score, he said, and would be for some time; importuned, he agreed to be at his apartment at six o'clock. Fox hung up, frowned at the transmitter for half a minute, dialed another number, and had better luck. Returning to his parked car, he drove to the offices of the Homicide Squad on Twentieth Street, sent his name in to Inspector Damon, and was admitted at once.

Anyone curious as to the true status of the police investigation of the Dunham murder would have needed only to observe Inspector Damon's reception of Tecumseh Fox. He got up and came around his desk to greet the visitor and shook hands as if he meant it.

Fox smiled at him. "My lord, is it as bad as that?"

"Everything's always bad here." Damon waved him to a chair. "All we get is crime. Something on your mind?"

"Nope. I'm in a mental blackout. I'm sorry if you thought I was Santa Claus. How's the Dunham case getting along?"

"Fine. Who wants to know?"

"Me and my employer. I've got a job." Fox took an envelope from his pocket, extracted a sheet of notepaper, and handed it over. "You'll be pleased to know that at least I was able to persuade Mrs. Pomfret not to have you fired."

Damon took in the brief note with a glance. He handed it back, grunted, and regarded Fox grimly. "When you get the Dunham case cleaned up," he said sarcastically, "there's a stabbing up in Harlem you can have."

"Thanks. I'll get in touch with you. I just got that commission from Mrs. Pomfret an hour ago. There's no corking or covering involved; she wants to know who killed her son. That's straight. If you already know, I'll mail this back to her and go home. Do you?"

"They sell papers at the corner."

Fox frowned. "All right. But I don't think that's very profound. Have I ever gone around blowing lids off? When I got lucky and broke the Coromander case, did I—"

"You'll need plenty of luck to break this one, my boy."

"Then you haven't opened a seam yet?"

"I have not. I know just exactly as much about who killed Dunham as I did when I walked in there a week ago yesterday. The papers think there's been a hush, but there hasn't. It's simply a case of somebody being either damn clever or damn lucky. We've tried everything. I don't need to tell you what we've done; you know what we do."

"I thought maybe you had it lined up but were short on proof."

"Proof?" Damon was bitter. "Hell, we haven't even got to the guessing stage."

"Have you got a few minutes to talk about it?"

"I never have a few minutes, but I'll talk about it. What do you want to know?"

The "few minutes" stretched into nearly an hour, but when Fox left, at a quarter to six, returned to his car and headed back uptown, all he had to show for it was additional material for a student of mankind. The salient and interesting items were assorted in his head:

### Adolph Koch

Wealthy bachelor businessman, 52, reputation good. Generous help to painters, writers, musicians. Also generous to young women. *Quid pro quo*. Tusar in his way—Hebe Heath? And Dunham knew it? No other motive.

### Ted Gill

Successful publicity agent, 30, reputation good. Arrested 1938, charged with assault by theatrical producer, acquitted. Sore at Tusar for not having picture taken with Hebe? Very thin—no other motive.

### Garda Tusar

Came to U.S. in 1933 with brother, 26. Lied about job, hasn't had one for three years. N.V.M.S. Lives expensively—at least $10,000 a year. Source of income—Perry Dunham? Unable to verify. Loved her brother but on bad terms with him recently. No motive to kill him or Dunham. Evasive, slippery, clever.

### Dora Mowbray

Pianist, 20, teaching for a living since father's death. Thought father was murdered, perhaps still does. Says Tusar left two notes. Motive against Tusar, avenging father's death. Against Dunham, fear of disclosure (this for everyone).

### Mrs. Pomfret

45. Large fortune intact. Possibly wished to ruin Tusar, had quarreled with him, but would not have harmed Perry. Lavish with money for Perry.

### Felix Beck

Top-flight teacher of violin, 61, married, two children, reputation good, finances fair. Bets on horse races. No motive.

### Henry Pomfret

Formerly U.S. diplomatic service, married Mrs. Pomfret (then Dunham) in Rome, 1932. 41. Clean record. No private income. Mutual dislike him and Perry (motive?). Thin. No hint Perry serious threat to him. No motive Tusar. No spending habits, apparently has little to spend. Wins at bridge at the Dummy Club.

### Hebe Heath

Born Mabel Daggett at Columbus, Ohio, 1915. Married 1936 to Los Angeles lawyer, divorced 1938. Nut. Arrested Santa Barbara 1938 for driving car into post office. Arrested Chicago 1939 for breaking man's nose with tennis racket. Chased Jan Tusar since August, 1939. Motive Tusar, pique, resentment, desire to humiliate. Pathological? Dr. Unwin interviewed her, hedged.

### Diego Zorilla

Formerly ranking concert violinist, fingers lost in accident ruined career. 34. Salary $140 a week music arranger MBC. Reputation good. Jilted by Garda Tusar in 1935. Old friend of Tusar. Embittered envy? Motive Dunham, yes, if he still loves G.T., and Dunham was keeping her.

For the rest, only a disheartening row of negations. No trail found from a purchase of potassium cyanide. No fingerprints on the paper container of the poison or the fragments of the whisky bottle picked up in the street corner, except, in the case of the bottle, those of Schaeffer and Perry Dunham. No trail from a purchase of varnish, nor evidence of its possession. No significant result from four days' surveillance of all those involved, abandoned after vigorous protests from Adolph Koch and Henry Pomfret. No hint of hidden designs, desires, intrigues, motives....No this, no that....

Fox was beginning to feel that he would indeed need

plenty of luck, and as he rolled uptown with the traffic he was not voicing his favorite battle cry.

As it happened, luck was on the job. He would have been willing to call it luck, though what really saved him was an inborn wariness, a hair-trigger alertness of his nerves which communicated to him a warning a split second sooner than the normally equipped man would have got it. Arriving at Diego's address promptly at six o'clock, he found it unnecessary to push a button in the vestibule, since the door was left unlocked to permit public access to a little optician's shop on the ground floor. That was not worthy of remark, but, mounting the two flights to the door of Diego's apartment, he found something that was. The door was not only unlocked, but was ajar a few inches, and his quick-accustomed eye caught in its first glance the bruised and splintered edge of the jamb which suggested that the door had been opened without the convenience of a key. Lifting his brows at it, he pushed the button and heard a bell ring inside—but nothing else. He pushed the button again, and go no response. He called out:

"Hey, Diego!"

Silence.

He lifted his hand to push the door open; but that was where the luck, or his inborn wariness, entered. He couldn't draw his pistol, for he was unarmed; but an elementary precaution could do no harm. He flattened himself against the wall to the right of the door at the hinge side, reached out to the nearest panel, and pushed.


11


DESPITE HIS prudence, what happened startled him because it was totally unexpected. As the door swung open there was a clatter, a spattering of liquid, another clatter as something hit the floor. Fox was six feet from the door—a good sidewise leap. As a pungent penetrating ordor reached his nostrils he backed away another six feet, and stood there glaring incredulously at a little enameled metal pan that had rolled into the hall when a voice came from his rear:

"Hello, sorry I'm a little late." It was Diego's bass rumble. "I've been—Hey, the door's open? What—"

Fox grabbed his arm. "Take it easy. We'd better back off a little."

"What the hell—"

Fox held him back. "You'd never believe it. I wouldn't if I hadn't seen it. I suppose it's been five thousand years since a kid first fixed a bowl of water to fall on grandpa's head when he opened a door. Only that's not water. It's either hydrocyanic or nitrobenzene, and if it's the latter the less we breathe the better we'll feel. I got here four minutes ago. The door had been pried open and was standing ajar. After ringing and yelling and getting no answer, I cautiously gave a push and that pan tumbled down, spilling enough to kill a horse if it landed on him."

Diego stared. "Kill?"

"Yes. If it's nitrobenzene. That stuff is as toxic as a volley from a machine gun and penetrates about as fast."

Diego stared down at the pan on the floor, at damp spots on either side of the threshold, and growled in his throat. "I'm going in and see—"

"Okay, if you've got good soles on your shoes and don't step in a puddle and keep moving. The fumes can get you. Don't touch that pan. Don't touch anything near the door."

Diego obeyed. He avoided the damp spots and halted only when he was in the middle of the living room. Fox went farther, to the windows opposite, and threw them both wide open. When he turned Diego was glowering around.

"Someone's been in here."

"Under the circumstances," Fox observed dryly, "that isn't much of a surprise."

"No, but look at those bookshelves."

Fox had already seen them on his trip across the room.

Half the books were lying on the floor. Other things were disarranged. Two drawers of a chest were standing open, and Diego was striding over to them. Fox went to the bathroom, opened the closet door and inspected the shelves there, returned to the living room, and saw that Diego had dropped into a chair, his face a black cloud, his white teeth gripping his lower lip.

"That vase," Fox said. "It's not where it was. Did you put it somewhere else?"

Diego made no reply.

"Don't be a sap." Fox sounded exasperated. "I know it's the Wan Li that was stolen from Pomfret. I knew it as soon as I saw it."

Diego goggled at him. "How could you? You'd never seen it."

"I'd seen a picture of it, and I know something about pottery. Did you put it somewhere else?"

"Yes. I put it—" Diego stopped. In a moment he went on:"What the hell. It's gone. I put it in that top drawer and locked it and it's been jimmied open and it's gone."

"Well." Fox crossed to a chair near a window and sat down. "I see." He started to hum, in an undertone, "The Parade of the Wooden Soldiers."

Diego barked, "Shut up!"

Fox looked startled and apologetic. "Was I doing that again? Excuse me. Well, it's gone. The vase. If you had arrived here before I did, and shoved the door open in the usual way, you would be gone too. Or going. So I saved your life. Does that appeal to you? By the way, do you want me to call the police or will you?"

"What are you talking about? Why should I call the police?"

"My lord," Fox said mildly. "Burglary? Grand larceny? Attempted murder?"

Diego's head fell till his chin touched his chest. His hands between his knees, he rubbed the palms together, up and down. Fox waited. Diego shook his head, without lifting it:

"I don't believe that. That stuff wouldn't kill a man.

"That's a question for the police, Diego."

"They wouldn't—I don't want the police." Diego raised his head. "This is my place, isn't it? That was broken into? And it was me who was expected to open that door, wasn't it?"

"Presumably." Fox's tone sharpened. "But not to a certainty. You knew I was coming here at six o'clock. You knew it at a quarter to five. That gave you plenty of time to get over here and make arrangements. In case my discovery of the vase had made you fear I might become a serious annoyance."

Diego was gazing at him, speechless. He found speech only to pronounce, in disbelief and withering scorn, a completely unprintable word.

Fox met his gaze and said calmly. "That's the way it is, Diego. That's exactly the way it is. There are eight of you, and one of you is a sneak and a snake and a murderer. And damn dangerous. And damn cunning. And a person of imagination. That varnish in Tusar's violin is about tops in my experience. Or bottom. I doubt if it's you, but if it is, I'm after you and I'll get you. A matter of business—I'm working for Mrs. Pomfret. And if it isn't here are some questions I want answers to. One, are you in love with Garda Tusar? Two, what do you know of her relations with any man or men, including Perry Dunham? Three, where did you get that vase? Four, who is it that wants to kill you, and why? We'll start with the simplest one. Where did you get the vase?"

Diego blurted harshly, "No one wants to kill me!"

"Then take the alternative. Why did you try to kill me?"

Diego opened his mouth, and shut it without speaking. He gazed in silence at Fox, at the drawer still standing open, at the door still swung wide with its splintered edge plainly visible. He took a deep spasmodic breath that shook his torso, and when that convulsion had passed fastened his eyes on Fox again.

"All right," he said, "get the police. I knew you knew that was Pomfret's vase. I knew that was why you wanted to see me today, to ask me to explain. The only explanation I could give was to admit that I stole it, which I didn't care to do. So I—as you say, I made arrangements. I might have known you wouldn't be caught in a booby trap like that."

"Then a few minutes after I had entered you ran up to make sure it had worked."

"Yes, I—to see if you—to see what—"

"You certainly are a champion goof, Diego."

"I know I am. Why I ever stole it in the first place—"

"Yeah. That was ill-advised. And now you are up against it, or will be when the cops get at you. Where did you get the nitrobenzene? You'll have to prove that, of course. And the pan? Weren't you at your office from the time I phoned until you left to come here? Why did you burglarize the door, why didn't you just use your key? The same with the drawer. And what did you do with the vase? I could go on for an hour. The dumbest cop in the world would give you the horse laugh."

"Let them," Diego said doggedly.

"My God," Fox protested in a tone of disgust, "you don't mean to say that you actually expect anyone to swallow that!"

"I mean," said Diego, meeting his gaze unwaveringly, "that if you call the police on this that's all they'll get from me." His face twisted with an involuntary grimace, showing his white teeth and his gums. "And anyone else. Includimg you. If you want to investigate a murder, that's all right, I want that as much as you do, but not here. I'm not a murderer. Damn you! What has my feeling for Garda got to do with murder? Or that goddam vase?"

Diego stopped; his jaw worked; he lifted a hand and let it drop again. "I'm sorry, Fox," he said with an odd and clumsy courtesy. "You think you saved my life. Thank you. That's all I'm going to say. To anyone." He pointed. "There's the phone over there."

Fox looked at him, at the crooked set to his mouth, at his narrowed eyes, half closed to conceal the mortal hurt to pride or hope or self-respect that had desperately moved him even to the ignominy of falsely declaring himself a thief. It was manifestly useless to badger him or wheedle him or reason with him; another time, another day, perhaps; not now. His hands were moving, and Fox, glancing there, saw that the tips of the index and middle fingers of his right hand were making little circles on the ends of the two stubs on the other hand. Fox had never seen him do that before; in fact, no one had; Diego had never permitted himself to indulge in that little gesture except in solitude.

Fox got up and went to the table and tore a piece from a newspaper, went to the hall and used the scrap of paper to pick up the pan, returned and put the pan on the table, and got his hat from the top of the chest of drawers. As he stopped in front of Diego, Diego looked up at him and then down again.

"Don't touch that pan with your bare fingers," Fox said. "That stuff is oily. Even one drop of it is dangerous. On your skin. It wouldn't kill you, but it might make you pretty sick. Get rubber gloves and wet a cloth with cleaning alcohol and wipe the floor and the door and the woodwork. Clean the pan with alcohol before you throw it away—unless you want to keep it for a souvenir. You can't lock the door, the lock's ruined. Some one tried to kill you and may try again. Don't be a damn fool."

"The police," Diego said. "I don't expect—I'm not asking any favors. I'm perfectly willing—"

"The police are busy on a stabbing up in Harlem," Fox said roughly, and strode out, down the stairs, and to the street.

## 12

IN A little restaurant on 54th Street west of Lexington Fox considered the situation, meanwhile disposing of some excellent oysters, good tender calf's liver, tolerable lyonnaise potatoes, and broccoli that was saved from being seaweed only by its color.

At the end of the oysters he went to the phone booth,

called Dora Mowbray's number, and got no answer. In the
middle of the liver he tried another number, that of Garda
Tusar in an apartment house on Madison Avenue, with the
same result. Before putting sugar in his coffee he tried still
another, Adolph Koch's residence on 12th Street, and was
informed by the soft voice of a colored maid that Mr. Koch
was out.

None of those disappointments was the quietus of a
brilliant idea. He had no brilliant ideas. There was no
sense in plodding along the trails, any of them, already
worn by the trampling of Inspector Damon's battalions—as,
for instance, the matter of Garda Tusar's income. That sort
of thing was pie for a good detective squad, and Damon
had fully realized the possibilities it offered of opening a
crack, but he had got nowhere. If Garda had been a
frequent visitor, discreet or indiscreet, to Koch's place, or
to Diego's or Perry Dunham's; or if one of them or any
other remunerative male had enjoyed recurrent hospitality
at her apartment; or if she had been habitually either
guest or hostess at some clandestine pied-à-terre—all those
possibilities had been explored by Damon's men with
painstaking and elaborate thoroughness, and Garda's mysterious opulence remained a mystery. The inevitable official conjecture, that she was blackmailing somebody, was
certainly plausible, but on that too there was a painful and
persistent lack of evidence.

It was the same with all the other traditionally indicated
lines of inquiry. In dogged desperation Damon had even
nosed into the matter of Lawrence Mowbray's death four
months previously, but had found nothing in that hole
either. Alone in his office on the twentieth floor of a
building on 48th Street, at 5:37 P.M. on November 29th,
Mowbray had toppled from a window, bounced from a
ledge eighty feet down, and smashed on the pavement.
The routine investigation had disclosed that Jan Tusar had
entered the building two or three minutes later and taken
an elevator to the twentieth floor, to keep an appointment
with Mowbray, but that was the only item of the record
which might have possessed significance, and it had none
for the present problem.

No, Fox decided as he set down his empty coffee cup and scowled at it, it was hopeless to start barking at the tails of the trained dogs. What was needed was a flash of inspiration, and the devil of it was that none came. All he could do was poke around somewhere and wait for it, and as good a place to poke as any was Perry Dunham's place on 51st Street, for which he had a key. There would even be a bed there which he might as well use. He paid his check, went to the phone booth again, asked for Brewster 8000, and after a little wait heard a familiar voice.

"Mrs. Trimble? Fox. Please tell Pokorny the billiard date is off because I won't get home tonight. And tell Sam to leave the strawberries until I get a look at them. I hope to be there tomorrow evening. Everything all right?"

"Fine." Mrs. Trimble had her mouth too close to the transmitter, and talked too loud, as usual. "Mr. Crocker skinned his leg a little and two pigs got out. They's a telegram."

"Telegram? From that fellow in Boston?"

"Not Boston, New York. Wait till I get it, Sam wrote it down." An interval, then her voice again: "It's from a woman, anyway it's signed Dora Mowbray: D, O—"

"I know. What does it say?"

"It says, 'Telegram received. Will arrive Brewster 8:48 as requested.'"

Fox missed a breath. "Read it again."

She repeated it.

"What time did it come?"

"Sam wrote it down. At 7:15."

"Hold the wire." Fox put the receiver on the shelf, whisked papers from his pocket, found a timetable among them and ran his eye down a column of it, glanced at his wrist watch, picked up the phone and told it, "All right, Mrs. Trimble, good-bye," and shot from the booth. Grabbing his hat and coat, and narrowly avoiding collisions with two startled waiters, he made for the street. Luckily there had been a space for his car near the entrance, and, running to it, he scrambled in, got it started, and jerked it into the lane.

Though it would take precious minutes to go crosstown,

the West Side Highway was his only hope, and he swung
into 57th Street and headed for it. Nothing much could be
done for that stretch, with a light and a stream of traffic at
every avenue; the Wethersill was no better than any old
jalopy; instead of fretting about it, he calculated. A part of
the timetable column was in his head:

| | |
|---|---|
| Bedford Hills ..................................... | 8:23 |
| Katonah ............................................ | 8:27 |
| Golden's Bridge ................................ | 8:32 |
| Purdy's ............................................. | 8:37 |
| Croton Falls ..................................... | 8:41 |
| Brewster ........................................... | 8:48 |

At Eighth Avenue his dashboard clock said 7:55.
Then either Bedford Hills or Katonah was out of the
question. Golden's Bridge, barely possible. Purdy's, possible. Croton Falls, yes, with luck. Brewster itself, of
course, but he didn't like that. He wanted to be on that
train, and find her, before it reached Brewster. The person
who had got her on that train by sending her a telegram
signed Tecumseh Fox had probably concocted a stratagem
that would get her off of it this side of Brewster.

Purdy's, possible.

Ninth Avenue...Tenth...Eleventh...he circled to the
ramp, shot up to the highway, and accelerated.

The only problem was cops, and that was a simple one.
As every motorist knows, there are two ways to avoid
trouble with cops: drive so slow they don't stop you, or so
fast they can't catch you. The second was no good for the
West Side Highway, since a phone call to the toll booths at
the Henry Hudson Bridge would have caught him, so Fox
gritted his teeth and held it under sixty, weaving smoothly
and expertly through the crowd holding to the conventional forty-five.

Half a mile beyond the toll gate his speedometer said
90. That, he thought, would do; and even at 90, on the
curves and dips of the rolling parkway, the rubber screamed
in protest at the outrageous imposition. On the curves all
of Fox was in his fingers on the wheel; on the infrequent

straightaways he could spare an instant for a glance in the driving mirror. The sign marking the city limits flashed by and he was on the Saw Mill River Parkway. He stepped it up to 95, and while the tires sang the engine lifted the long car over a sharp rise like a swallow enjoying its wings. As he flew under the Crestwood light his clock said 8:19. Purdy's still possible, so at Hawthorne Circle he would take Route 22.

But he didn't. Neither the cop nor the curve at the circle would like anything over 50, so on the approach he lifted his toe; then suddenly, getting nearer, he pressed it down again and put a thumb on the horn button and kept it there. His headlights had picked up the cop, who, instead of loafing near the police booth as was customary, was standing in the middle of the roadway waving both arms. Fox set his jaw, gripped the wheel, kept the horn going, fed gas, and aimed straight for the cop. When the cop jumped, with nothing to spare, he jumped left, and Fox swerved right. Then he pulled it sharp left for the circle, swayed, and was on two wheels, the tires shrieking, got on all four again, and jerked straight into the Bronx River Parkway Extension.

Of course there would be more phoning ahead, this time doubtless to the State Barracks near Pleasantville, and in three minutes the parkway would be too hot for him. So in two minutes he left it, swinging right onto a bumpy country road. He thought it would take him straight to Armonk, but it didn't take him straight anywhere; at a fork he had to guess, bumped along in all directions for another two miles, and finally had to ask a boy the way to Route 22. When at length he got to it, Purdy's was not even a hope.

On that narrow curving route it took more driving, and he gave it all he had. Near Bedford Hills he missed a car emerging from a driveway only by taking to the grass on the other side and grazing a pole. At Katonah his clock said 8:35; the train had been and gone eight minutes earlier. At Golden's Bridge he had cut it down to five minutes. He rocketed through Purdy's at 8:39, stepped it up a little, lost traction on a downhill curve, got a wheel in

the ditch and miraculously made the road again, and heard
the train whistle for Croton Falls. One minute later he
turned off onto gravel, scooted downgrade to the Croton
Falls station and jerked to a stop, tumbled out and ran,
and grabbed the step rail of the vestibule of the last coach
and swung himself on board.

He was sickeningly certain he had made a fool of
himself; surely, by some ruse or other, she had been taken
off before now. If so...

He opened the door to the rear coach and entered. It
was the smoker, and was nearly empty, since the train was
nearing the end of its run, and of the seven or eight
passengers in sight none was female. In the next coach
ahead there were three women, but a glance at the backs
of their heads, all that showed from the rear, was enough
to eliminate them; nevertheless, as he strode up the aisle,
he turned his head for glimpses of faces. There were only
two more chances.

He used but one. Three paces inside the next coach, he
saw her. He stopped and stared, bracing himself against a
seat as the train lurched around a curve. Yes. She was in
profile, her head turned to look at the traveling companion
who was speaking to her. Fox moved on up the aisle; but
even when he halted beside the seat immediately back of
them, no notice was taken of him. He stood and glared
down at them. He could actually see the soft light that
shone in Dora's eyes, but they were oblivious of him; and
the beatified murmur of Ted Gill's voice as he gazed back
at her....

Fox was close enough to touch them....

From the end of the coach a trainman sang out: "Brewster!"

"Oh," Dora said, "he said Brewster." Ted nodded, heaved
a sigh which indicated that he had been neglecting his
breathing, tore his eyes loose, stood up to reach for the
coat rack, became aware of surveillance, turned his head,
and said calmly and imperturbably:

"Hello."

Dora's glance came up over the back of the seat. "Why,
hello there!"

Fox slowly shook his head. "Holy Saint Peter."

"We're getting off at Brewster," Ted announced, handling Dora's coat as if it were made of angel down and star dust.

"Correct," Fox said grimly. "We're there. Go ahead and get your things on."

The train rolled alongside the station and jerked to a stop. Fox followed them up the aisle and down the steps to the platform. A raw wind was blowing and a few snowflakes were dancing around the globes of the platform lights, and Ted hurried Dora inside the station. Fox was impeded for a moment by a man who wanted to greet him, and when he rejoined the couple over by a window Ted was saying to Dora:

"This is the first place we ever went together. Brewster. But not the last. It's a nice little station. Very nice."

"Well?" Fox demanded.

Dora smiled at him.

"Oh, yes," Ted said affably, recollecting him. "I guess I owe you an explanation. Did you get a telegram?"

"I did. Acknowledging one I had sent to Miss Mowbray."

"That's right. Only it was me that sent it. Lucky coincidence your being on the same train. You see, I figured she probably wouldn't wire an answer, she'd just take the train I told her to take, because I told her it was something very urgent—"

"And signed my name."

"I wrote it on the telegram, sure. I had to. I thought you'd never even know about it, and you wouldn't have if she hadn't wired a reply. The trouble was, she wouldn't let me see her. She wouldn't let me talk to her. She sent back a letter I wrote her. She misunderstood about my going to Mexico to get Hebe. I knew—well, I didn't know, but I hoped—if I got her some place like on a train—you see, she thought I was a lousy tramp—"

"I did not," Dora denied. "I merely thought—"

"Excuse me," Fox said dryly. "You've had an hour and a half for that. I doubt if your minds are in any condition to deal with externals, but it wasn't a lucky coincidence that I was told about the telegram, and I drove from 57th Street to Croton Falls in forty-four minutes. The cop at Hawthorne

Circle is alive only because he didn't jump a tenth of a second too late; I risked that. At a hundred miles an hour I missed a car coming out of a driveway by maybe three inches."

"Gosh," Ted said cheerfully, "good thing you missed him!"

"I wish I'd been with you," Dora declared. "I've always wanted to drive like that, just once."

"You do?" Ted asked her reproachfully. "You wish you'd been with him, do you?"

"Well—" Their eyes met, and clung. "I wish I had a twin and she was with him."

It was obviously hopeless; their cerebrums had entirely suspended operations. They were blissfully incapable of understanding why news of the telegram had caused Fox to risk life and limb and make his car a deadly menace over fifty miles of highway and byway; the question didn't even occur to them.

He demanded, "What are you going to do now?"

"Oh," Ted said, "there's a train back at ten thirty. We'll take a walk or fool around..."

"That's a good idea. Take a long walk. You may get lost and starve to death."

Fox marched for the door on the street side, debouched, found his friend Joe Prisco, the taxi man, and asked to be driven to Croton Falls. When they got there a brief inspection of the Wethersill disclosed no marks of battle except scratched paint where the rear fender had grazed the pole.

"You ought to be more careful," Joe admonished him.

"Yeah, I'm going to be," Fox agreed.

Heading towards New York, he left Route 22 at the first intersection, worked east, and eventually made the Hutchinson River Parkway. That way he didn't go within miles of Hawthorne Circle. Idling along at 50, he invited his nerves to calm down a little, but they ignored the invitation. They had prepared themselves for an explosion of energy, and all they were getting was an evening ride in the country.

It was a quarter to eleven when, having left the car at a
garage, he arrived at the address on 51st Street where
Perry Dunham had maintained a bachelor apartment.
There he encountered a fresh irritation in the shape of a
sour and suspicious hallman, who, not satisfied by Fox's
possession of the key and the note signed by Mrs. Pomfret, insisted on communicating with the police; and since
the matter had to be referred to Inspector Damon and he
was not on duty, it was necessary to phone him at home.
At length the hurdle was cleared, and Fox was taken in an
elevator to the sixth floor and directed to a door. He
opened it with the key, entered and found light switches
and flipped them, and gazed around in blank astonismment.

"I suppose," he muttered sarcastically, "it was Ted Gill
looking for a telegraph blank."

There was a phone on a table by the opposite wall.
Dodging obstacles, he crossed to it, found it was connected, and asked for a number. After a wait he responded to a
hello:

"Inspector Damon? Tecumseh Fox. I'm sorry to disturb
you again, but whoever worked Dunham's apartment
neglected to straighten up. I never saw such a mess, books
and things all over the floor, cushions slashed open—
What? No. I don't know, I just came in. Sure. Okay."

He stood and glared around at the indescribable jumble. This was where he had intended to spend a restful
night after an hour or so of leisurely inspection. A feather,
one of thousands out of the cushions, was clinging to the
cuff of his trousers, and he plucked it off and puffed it into
the air. There was no bed in sight. He went to a door that
was standing ajar, passed through, and discovered a bed,
but not in a condition to invite repose. The covers were
strewn around, and the mattress was in the middle of the
floor with its ticking ripped off and its insides scattered in
all directions. He returned to the other room and made a
tour, looking, but not touching anything. He would have
liked to rescue a copy of *Inside Asia* that was sprawling in
a heap of other books, its leaves crumpled, but forbore.
He saw *The Grapes of Wrath; Rouge et Noir; The Mason*

*Wasps*—apparently Dunham's tastes had ranged—*Madame Recamier; No Arms, No Armour; Thomas Bissell Old Coins Catalogue No. 38*—

He frowned down at the last, emitted a grunt, and stooped and picked it up. Leafing through it, he found that it was merely what its cover indicated: a catalogue of old and rare coins, with pictures of some and prices of many. Coenwulf of Britain, 9th century. Byzantine coin of Andronicus II. The Great Mogul Jahangir....

When Sergeant Craig arrived with men and equipment thirty minutes later, Fox was still learning things about old and rare coins. He greeted the sergeant and wished him luck, told him that his fingerprints would be found on the coin catalogue but on nothing else except the telephone, and left him to his laborious and probably fruitless task. He had it in mind to stop downstairs for some queries regarding recent visitors to the Dunham apartment, but found that he had been forestalled by two plain-clothes men who had the acidulous hallman in a corner and were thrusting their jaws out at him, so he departed, walked six blocks to the Sherman Hotel, got a room, and went to bed.

In the morning he had his choice of several moves, all obvious and uninspired, and none promising. He settled, not wholly by contrariety, on the least obvious. The weakest link in the official chain of negatives, judging from Damon's sketchy report the previous afternoon, was that dealing with the ménage of Adolph Koch, with particular reference to visitors resembling Garda Tusar; and Fox, having spoken with the maid on the telephone and appraised her from her voice, decided to test that link. It would of course be desirable not to arrive until after Koch had left for his office, so he went uptown first for a brief call on Mrs. Pomfret, where he learned nothing new except that her son Perry, as far as she was aware, had not collected old and rare coins or displayed any interest in them.

But though it was after ten o'clock when he arrived at the Koch house on 12th Street, it was still too early. He never got to see the maid at all. The large and dignified colored man who opened the door informed him, to his chagrin, that Mr. Koch was at home; and, after asking him to wait, returned shortly and conducted him to a door in the rear and bowed him through.

Koch, putting something down on a table, came toward him to shake hands. As Fox met him and they exchanged greetings, a buzzer sounded.

"Damn it," Koch said, "I might as well be the office boy. Excuse me."

He went to a telephone the other side of the table and answered it, waving Fox to a chair. Fox sat down and looked around, as one does during a phone conversation that is none of one's business. It was a solid and attractive room, subdued as to color, with comfortable chairs, handsome rugs, a large cabinet of pottery at one end and the walls of two sides lined with books...

It was as Fox's eyes were traveling to the other wall that they stopped and fastened themselves to one spot. It was occupied by the object which Koch had been depositing on the table when he entered; and the object—yes, his eyes told him, indubitably—was the Wan Li black rectangular vase which he had last seen behind a pile of washcloths in Diego's bathroom closet.

## 13

FOX LOOKED in another direction, with, he hoped, no gleam in his eye.

Koch finished with the phone, pushed it away, and dropped into a chair.

"You would suppose," he observed testily, "that a man's business might run itself for an hour or two. It's my own fault, letting them depend on me for everything, so when I don't get there sharp at nine thirty as usual..." He shrugged. "What can I do for you?"

"I'm out fishing." Fox smiled at him. "Mrs. Pomfret got

impatient and hired me to find out who killed her son."

"Ah." Koch smiled back. "She would."

"And I'm trying to get a rise somewhere."

Koch's brows went up. "From me?"

"From anyone. I'm not particular."

"Then the police haven't made much progress?"

"Nothing very notable." Fox threw one knee over the other. "By the way, you were speaking of your business—I know you make women's clothes—do you make fabrics too? I have a note here from Mrs. Pomfret, if you'd care to see it, requesting co-operation—"

"That's all right." Koch waved it away. "You couldn't be as objectionable as the police have been even if you tried. Nor as clumsy, I hope. They've been pumping my servants about the guests I invite to my house." He smiled. "Yes, we manufacture some of our own fabrics. Does that have some sinister significance?" His eyes looked amused.

"I wouldn't say sinister. Do you dye your fabrics?"

"Certainly."

"Aniline dyes?"

"Of course. Everybody does." Koch's brow showed a crease. "I guess I'm up with you, but I don't see the point. If you're delicately leading up to nitrobenzene, we have gallons of it, and it smells like hydrocyanic, but after all it was hydrocyanic that was put in Perry's whisky. Wasn't it?"

"Sure. I told you I'm just fishing. Do you happen to know that nitrobenzene spilled on a man, even on his clothing, can kill him?"

"I don't 'happen' to know it. I do know it. Anyone does who makes aniline dyes." Koch was frowning. "What the devil is this, anyhow?"

"Nothing. Probably nothing important. A nosey detective asking mysterious questions. That is, it naturally seems mysterious to you...."

"It certainly does." Koch, still frowning, got up and stepped to the side of the table. "And speaking of mysteries, here's another one." He picked up the vase. "Look at that!"

Fox did so, without excessive interest. "It's pretty," he conceded. "What about it?"

"Pretty?" Koch stared at him, snorted, and passed caressing finger tips around the lip of the vase. "But I presume there are intelligent people who might call it 'pretty.' Do you remember, the other day at Mrs. Pomfret's, there was talk of a vase, a Wan Li rectangular, that had been stolen from Henry's collection? This is it!"

"Really?" Fox gawked at it. "That's interesting. Where did you get it?"

Koch replaced it gently on the table and grunted, "That's the mystery. It was delivered here this morning, by parcel post. Just as I was about to leave for the office. That's why you found me still here. I coveted that thing every time I saw it at Pomfret's, and you can imagine—when Williams brought it and showed it to me—he had already opened the package—"

Fox nodded. "Yes, I can imagine. Especially in view of the peculiar circumstances. What are you going to do with it?"

"Return it to its owner, damn it! I phoned him just before you came, and I'm going to take it up there now. If I kept it here twenty-four hours, the temptation—but you wouldn't understand. You called it 'pretty.' "

"I apologize," Fox said mildly, and added in the same tone, "This parcel post gambit is getting a little monotonous. Since you say it's a mystery, I suppose you don't know who sent it?"

"No."

"Was it addressed to you?"

"Certainly. This is my house." Koch pointed to articles on a chair by the wall: brown wrapping paper, and a sturdy little fiber carton which had started its career as a container of Dixie Brand Canned Tomatoes. "It came in that."

"May I take a look at it?" Fox went to the chair. He found it was unnecessary to spread the paper out to inspect the address, for it had been neatly folded so that a small printed label was in the center of the visible surface, as well as the postmark. Picking it up to examine the label more closely, he saw that it wasn't printed, but expensively and elegantly engraved, with Koch's name and address. He turned, his raised brows putting a question.

Koch nodded. "The beggar has a nerve, hasn't he?" He was suave and amused. "That was clipped from the corner of an envelope of my personal stationery and pasted on there. But it doesn't help much, because I'm pretty lavish with my stationery. Only last week I sent out a thousand invitations to a show of Frank Mitchell's—a young painter. I'm interested in." He glanced at his watch. "You know, I must be at my office before noon, and I do want to see the look on Pomfret's face when I hand him this thing. If you want to ask me some more mysterious questions, why don't you ride up there with me? Unless you'd rather stay and try to get more out of my servants than the police did?"

Was his smile banter, or a challenge, or merely the polite urbanity of a civilized man tolerating unmerited harassment? Fox couldn't tell; but in any case, it seemed doubtful that the maid was saving any helpful revelation for him. He accepted the invitation to accompany Koch uptown.

It appeared, during the twenty minute ride, that Koch had no revelations either. He could add nothing to what he had told the police and the district attorney. He had regarded Perry Dunham as a bumptious young scatter-brain, but he sympathized with Mrs. Pomfret and would be willing, he said, to undergo serious inconvenience if by doing so he could be of any help in the situation. He would like to know why the devil Fox had asked about nitrobenzene; he would also like to know who had sent him that vase, and why to him; he was in fact, he said, in a vastly better position for asking questions than for answering them.

The effect he produced at Pomfret's, as registered not only on the husband's face but also on the wife's, must have met his extreme expectations, when, after a brief and rather stilted exchange of amenities, he suddenly pro-duced the vase. Pomfret stared at it for five seconds in dazed incredulity, then stretched his mouth from ear to ear in a grin of unalloyed delight, and reached with an eager hand. Mrs. Pomfret, whose lids were even redder and more swollen, and skin more leaden, and shoulders less erect, than before, darted a sharp and suspicious glance at Koch, and one just as sharp, though not as suspicious, at Fox.

"That's the Wan Li, isn't it?" Koch inquired.

Pomfret gurgled an ecstatic affirmative.

Koch bowed to Mrs. Pomfret. "I couldn't resist giving myself the pleasure of delivering it in person. Now I have to rush to my office. Mr. Fox will explain to you."

He bowed again and was gone. Pomfret didn't even see him go; he was carefully and lovingly inspecting all sides of his treasure so miraculously returned; and though he presumably listened to Fox's recital of the circumstances of the vase's return, he didn't halt the examination for it. Mrs. Pomfret gave Fox both her ears and her eyes, and when he finished asked bluntly:

"Well, what do you think?"

Fox shrugged and turned up his palms.

"Fish," she said in weary derision. "There's no question that the Heath creature took it and he got it from her and mailed it to himself. Or else he took it in the first place and got frightened...." She fluttered a flabby hand. "It doesn't matter now." She pointed at the vase in her husband's hands. "I hate that thing now. I hate everything here. I hate everything. I hate life."

Pomfret hastily put the vase down and passed an arm around her shoulders. "Now, Irene," he expostulated gently, "you know very well that's morbid...."

Her lips tightened to a thin line, she reached for his hand and gripped the fingers till he winced. Fox arose, said he would communicate anything that was worth communicating, and took his departure.

The thing was as chaotic and senseless as a nightmare. As a nightmare, he thought, marching south on the avenue like a man knowing his destination, which he didn't—as the sort of nightmare Hebe Heath would have. Nothing led anywhere; nothing had any apparent relation to anything else. Take for instance that coin catalogue in Dunham's apartment. Or Dunham's going for the violin that day. Why? Granted that he knew the varnish was there, he couldn't very well have expected to scrape it out. Or take

that damned vase; was it connected with the death of
Perry Dunham or wasn't it, and if so, how? It would have
been reasonable to suppose that Mrs. Pomfret's suspicion
was sound, that the vase-lifting had been another exploit
of the wondrous and unimaginable Hebe—but in that
case, how in heaven's name had it got into Diego's closet,
and why should Diego?...

He swerved abruptly into a cigar store, sought the
phone booth and called the MBC studios, and after an
inquiry and a short wait heard Diego's bass rumble in his
ear.

"Diego? Tec Fox."

"Oh. Hello. How are you?"

"I'm fine. Will you have lunch with me?"

"Uh—I'm sorry. Uh—an engagement."

"Then later, five o'clock, whenever you say, for a drink?
And have dinner with me?"

"What do you want?"

"I want to talk with you."

"About that—thing?"

"Yes. That and other—"

"No." Diego was curt. "I won't talk about it, now or any
other time. That's definite and final."

"But Diego. I don't think you realize—"

The line was dead.

Fox stared at the soundless receiver in amazed disbelief.
Diego the courteous Spaniard, Diego of the quaint and
engaging punctilio, had hung up on him! He could almost
as soon have believed him capable of putting poison in a
man's whisky....With slow reluctance he replaced the
phone, sat there a moment frowning thoughtfully at it,
arose abruptly with an air of decision, strode out to the
sidewalk, and turned west at the next corner toward
Madison Avenue.

On Madison he went half a block downtown, entered
the somewhat gaudy lobby of an apartment hotel, crossed
to the elevator and stepped within, met the inquiring
glance of the operator and told him casually, "Ninth,
please." But it was not as simple as that. The operator
asked him politely but pointedly whom he was calling

on; and it turned out that his attempt to cut a corner had been unnecessary, for when the young man at the desk phoned Miss Tusar's apartment that Mr. Fox was calling he was instructed to send him up. Unobtrusively Fox was observing faces, knowing that all members of the staff from the manager down, questioned by the police regarding Miss Tusar, had displayed either a loyal reticence regarding their tenant's habits and movements and friends, or a surprising ignorance of them.

Similarly he observed the square and stolid countenance of the uniformed maid who admitted him to Suite D on the ninth floor. Her name and address—Frida Jurgens, 909 East 83rd Street—was in a notebook in his pocket, one of several procured the day before from Inspector Damon;and one glimpse of her obdurate geometrical visage was enough to explain the meagerness of her contribution to the dossier. With efficiency, if with no grace, she disposed of Fox's hat and coat and conducted him within.

Garda, advancing to meet Fox, greeted him with an extended hand, a half smile confined to a corner of her mouth, and the full direct regard of her black eyes, with now no blaze in them.

"It took you a long time to get around to it," she said with pretended petulance. "That's a better chair there. You remember you told Mrs. Pomfret you'd try to persuade me to be reasonable? That was more than a week ago." Sitting, she shivered delicately. "It seems a year. Doesn't it?"

Fox, taking the recommended chair, said that it did. So she was going to be amiable and charming, which she could do without straining at it. The chair was in fact comfortable, the room was not too hot and had air in it, the décor was tasteful and restrained....

"I don't know," Fox said, "about persuading you to be reasonable, but I'd like to persuade you to be frank. Henry Pomfret's Wan Li vase is back home again."

A flicker of her lids veiled the black eyes for an instant, then he had them back. "His vase? You mean the one that was stolen?"

"Yep, that one."

"It's back home? You mean he got it back? How nice!"
She was effusive. "Where did you find it?"

"Thanks for the compliment." Fox smiled at her.
"Undeserved. Mr. Koch returned it to him this morning."

"What!" Garda looked blank. "Koch!—How did he—my
God, Koch? He stole it? He had it all the time?"

"Not according to him," Fox said dryly. "He got it the
way Mrs. Pomfret got the violin back—it came by parcel
post. This morning. He spent an hour or so admiring it
and then delivered it to its owner. Pomfret is delighted."

"And Koch doesn't know who sent it to him?"

"Nope."

"And no one—then they've got it back but they don't
know who took it."

"That's right. They don't. But I think I do. I think you
took it."

Garda's eyes opened at him. The blaze was there for a
fleeting second, then she burst into laughter. It was not an
affected ripple or a forced haw-haw, but a real and hearty
laugh. She checked it, leaned forward and pursed her lips
prettily at Fox, and coaxed him in mock entreaty:

"Tell me another one! Oh, please!"

Fox shook his head. "That's the only one I know, Miss
Tusar. I'd like to enlarge on it. May I?"

"You may if you'll keep it funny." Garda had sobered.
"That's the first time I've laughed since—for a long time."

"I doubt if you'll find it funny. It's complicated, too. It
begins with a question the police have been trying to
answer, where your income comes from. Inspector Damon
says that you spend more than ten thousand a year,
probably a good deal more, that its source is not visible,
and that you decline to reveal it."

"Why should I? It's none of their business. Nor yours."

"That may be true. But that's the trouble with a criminal investigation: it tries every hole in sight until it finds
the one its rabbit is in, and that's often a serious inconvenience to innocent bystanders. I suppose you know that
the police have tested the theory that you are being
financed by some person—uh—"

"Don't spare my sensibilities," Garda snapped. "Of

course I know it. They've even tried to bully my maid."

"Sure. What do you expect? You're one of the central figures in a murder case, and you're concealing something. They conclude, since you won't tell the source of your income, that it must be either criminal or disgraceful, or both. The theory I spoke of—they haven't been able to get evidence of that, so they're trying another one. That you're blackmailing someone."

"They!..." Garda's eyes flashed. "They wouldn't dare!"

Fox nodded imperturbably. "That's what they're working on now. I doubt if they'll get anywhere. My own theory is that you're a bandit. I think you stole Pomfret's vase."

"That was funny the first time—"

"I didn't mean it to be. Please. Just let me sketch it. You are beautiful and clever, probably unscrupulous, and have entrée to places where there are all kinds of small and portable objects of considerable value. It would be no trick at all for you to realize considerably more than ten thousand a year. You took that vase of Pomfret's, knowing it was worth a lot of money, but had to hang onto it because you found it was impossible to dispose of it safely. Please, Miss Tusar, you might as well let me finish. Diego, who loved you and had been intimate with you, knew how you—made moey. He suspected, or even knew, that you had taken the vase, charged you with it, and compelled you to turn it over to him. He may have threatened to expose you, but if he did it was only a bluff, for Diego is too much of a gentleman to expose a lady bandit. Doubtless his intention was to return it to Pomfret, but being a simple soul, wholly devoid of the resources of an intriguer—"

"That's enough!" Garda's eyes were snapping. "To expect me to sit and listen to a rigmarole of lies—"

"Not all lies, Miss Tusar. It isn't a lie that Diego had the vase. I saw it there at his place."

Garda's lips parted, and Fox could hear the breath going in. There was no fire in her eyes; instead, they withdrew; the lids half closed, and the slits were dull dead-black. "I don't—" she began, and stopped.

Fox said patiently, "I saw the Wan Li vase in Diego's

closet. I assure you that isn't a lie. How it got from there
into a parcel-post package is another matter. I have an
assortment of theories on that, but they can wait. The
point now is, where did Diego get it? I'm convinced he
got it from you. In no other way can I account for his
having acted as he did to me. He did, didn't he, Miss
Tusar? He got the vase from you?"

Garda shook her head, but apparently not to signify a
simple negative, for a corner of her mouth curled upward
in disdain, half indignant and half amused. "Really?" she
said. "You really ask me if I am a common little thief, like
that? And if it were so? You would expect me—do you
know what?" Her eyes danced at him. "I have a notion to
say yes, and see what next you would say—" She stopped
abruptly, her whole expression changed, and she fairly
spat at him, "You are a complete fool!"

Fox sighed, gazed at her gloomily, and said nothing.

"Your Diego too!" Garda said harshly. "Speak of Diego!
He's your friend, no? And he had that vase? Why don't
you ask him where he got it? That would be a different
affair, now, if you bring him and he would lie and say he got
the vase from me—"

"Shut up!" Fox blurted at her savagely.

Instantly she smiled at him. "Ah," she said softly, "you
don't like—"

"I said shut up!" Fox was standing, towering over her,
his neck muscles twitching. "So if Diego said you had the
vase you'd call him a liar, would you? You may or may not
be a common little thief, I admit I can't prove it, but you're
certainly a common little rat!" She came up from her
chair; his hand roughly pushed her back; she smiled up at
him.

"I would enjoy," Fox said more quietly but not with any
less feeling, "rubbing that smile off. If it wasn't for Diego I
would. I like Diego. I might even say I love him if I hadn't
quit loving anybody whatever some years ago. I've been
hired by Mrs. Pomfret to investigate the murder of her
son. At the time I took the job I didn't think Diego could
possibly have been sneak enough to poison a man, but
since then I've learned about his infatuation for you, God

help him, and also about that vase. He won't tell me anything about the vase. I ask you about it, because if it had nothing to do with the death of Perry Dunham I can forget the damn thing and go on with the job I was hired for."

He pressed his hand harder on her shoulder, the fingers through the soft flesh to the bone. "Quit wriggling! I still can't believe that Diego poisoned Dunham, but it's possible. To protect you he might have done anything. If what you tell me about the vase makes it seem probable that he did, I'm out of it. If the police get him, then they do. I hope they don't. I'm not going to. You can take my word for that. So that's why I've got to know about the vase. Quit wriggling! If you have any sense—"

"Frida! Frida!"

Fox straightened up and folded his arms. From the other side of a door steps were heard, a little hurried but not precipitate; the door opened, and from the threshold the maid looked across at them, her phlegmatic facial geometry perfectly composed.

"Phone downstairs," Garda told her in a voice that was not quite steady, "and tell Mr. Thorne a man is here annoying me. Or—wait a minute—or get Mr. Fox's hat and coat." Her eyes darted to Fox. "Which would you prefer?"

"You're making a mistake. Perhaps a fatal one. If it's like this I'm going through with it."

Their eyes met. His were cold and hard; hers were hot, defiant, contemptuous.

"The hat and coat, Frida," she said.

"Then take what you get," Fox said with pale ferocity, and left her.

# 14

ON THE outside the old house on East 83rd Street, though not exactly disreputable, was certainly dingy and dirty; on the inside it was still dingy but not dirty at all. On the contrary, it was extremely clean. In the lower hall and dining room at nine thirty that Tuesday evening, there was a pervasive odor of pork cooked with sour cream. In the kitchen the odor pervaded not only the room but also the breath of Frida Jurgens, which was to be expected, since she had just completed the consumption of four of the fillets with trimmings. Usually she was fairly satisfied with what she had got at the apartment of her employer, but on Tuesday, the day her aunt Hilda had *Schweinsfilets mit sauer Sahne*, she always left plenty of room.

She put down her knife and fork and eructed with pure pleasure, and was in so benign a mood that when a voice sounded from the front calling her name no faintest sign of protest accompanied the pushing back of her chair.

In the dining room her aunt Hilda had turned on the light and was squinting defensively at a strange man standing with an enormous flat book under his arm. His appearance was at the same time comical and maleficent; the former chiefly by reason of slick oily hair parted in the middle and enormous black-rimmed spectacles, and the latter by a jagged livid scar that slanted from his right cheekbone to the corner of his mouth. He had put his hat on a corner of the dining table.

"Sinsuss man," Aunt Hilda hissed warningly at Frida.

"United States decennial census," the man said sternly, the distortion of his lips by the scar making it indescribably sardonic.

"The census?" Frida demanded. "Already? The paper and the radio both said April second."

"This," the man said scornfully, "is the prolegomenon. The radio explained that."

"I didn't hear it. And at night like this?"

"Well." The man leered at her. "If you wish me to report to the district administrator..."

"Now, now," Aunt Hilda said anxiously. Aunt Hilda was constitutionally anxious. "Report you by us? Now, now." She turned to Frida and sputtered a stream of German at her, and got a little of it back. At the end she told the man, "My niece speaks better English," and bustled out of the room. Frida pulled out two chairs, sat on one of them, clasped her hands on her lap, and said with no expression whatever, "My name is Frida Jurgens. I am a naturalized citizen—"

"Wait a minute, please." The man, sitting, got the book opened and cocked at an angle that kept its pages out of her range of vision. "First, the head of this household?"

Fifteen minutes later Frida was showing faint but unmistakable signs of strain. She had answered questions regarding two aunts, four cousins, and a brother who drove a taxicab, and the responsibility was heavy; for it was a general suspicion in that neighborhood that the census was some kind of a police trick and dire consequences might be expected. The trouble was her two cousins who belonged, as she knew, to a certain organization—she felt moisture on her forehead but dared not wipe it off—so when he finished with the others and began on her, her relief was so great that she failed to notice that the United States appeared to possess a greatly augmented curiosity in her particular case. Where was her present employement, how long had she been there, what was the nature of her duties, how many persons were there in the household, either constantly or occasionally, how many meals was she expected to prepare, what were her hours, how much time did she have off?...

She said she had plenty of time off, but just how much, it depended. The census taker declared, with a frown of dissatisfaction, that for the purpose of the employment census that was too vague. It depended on what?

"It depends on her," Frida told him. "She don't eat in much. When she don't, I leave at seven, sometimes even earlier. But then again she tells me to leave at two o'clock maybe, or in the morning even, and not to come back that day. So the time off is fine."

"How often does that happen?"

"Pretty often. Maybe a day in a week, maybe three days in a week."

"Certain days? Tuesdays for instance?"

"Oh, no, not certain days. Just days."

"How long has that been going on?"

"Ever since I'm working there. Over a year."

"When was the last time it happened?"

Frida frowned. "I don't lie," she said resentfully.

"Of course not. Why should you? When was the last time?"

"It was Friday. Last Friday."

"Perhaps Miss Tusar lets you go because she intends to go somewhere herself. She intends to be away and won't need you."

"Maybe. She don't say!"

"Does she go out, or make preparations to go, before you leave?"

"No, she don't."

"Does she tell you about it in advance? Say the day before?"

"No. It mostly happens all of a sudden. Soon after Mr. Fish phones."

"Fish?" The census man uttered a sociable little laugh. "That always strikes me as a funny name. I know a fellow named Fish, a short fat man with a double chin. I don't think it would be him phoning Miss Tusar, though. Is it? Short and fat with a double chin?"

"I don't know. I never saw him. I answer the phone and he says to tell Miss Tusar Mr. Fish wants to speak to her, and I tell her."

"And soon after, she tells you you can have the rest of the day off."

"Yes, sir."

"It's a funny world."

Frida agreed to that with a nod. The census man asked her a few more questions, more as a friend than an inquisitor, closed his book and arose and got his hat, and departed. Without, he marched to the corner and entered a Bar & Grill and sought a phone booth, dialed a number, and spoke:

"Inspector Damon? Tecumseh Fox. Regrettable news. The lobby and elevator staff of the Bolton Apartments have been holding out on you. A man whose name may or may not be Fish has been calling on Miss Tusar once or twice or thrice a week for over a year. I should say it calls for suasion. How about gathering them in? Right. I'll be there in about half an hour."

At a moment well past midnight the atmosphere of Room Nine in the basement of police headquarters was permeated with tobacco smoke and ill humor. A dozen men of various ages and appearances and emotional conditions were on a row of wooden chairs at one end of the large room. Four or five plain-clothesmen sat or stood around. Inspector Damon braced his fundament on the edge of a rough wooden table and looked morose. Tecumseh Fox, his hair no longer slick and oily and the scar and spectacles gone, was at a water cooler in a corner taking a drink.

The suasion, which had been forceful in spots though never violent, had been totally unproductive. The manager, the assistant manager, the doormen, the hallmen, the elevator men, all maintained that they had never seen or heard of a Mr. Fish, that Miss Tusar had no habitual or even frequent visitor, male or female, that they wouldn't dream of withholding evidence from the police and that they wanted to go home. That had been going on for over two hours.

Damon crossed over to the corner where Fox was. "We might as well let them go," he muttered digustedly. "They're all lying. Or the maid invented Mr. Fish. Or Miss Tusar postponed her preparations for going out until after the maid had left. Take your pick."

Fox shook his head. "You've left out one. Since they're here we might as well try it. Maybe they're all telling the truth for a change, including the maid. When is a Fish not a Fish?"

Damon grunted. "You mean he gave another name and pretended he was calling on someone else? But we've already—"

"Nope. Who could enter as often as he pleased, and go up in the elevator, without giving his name at all?"

"I don't— Oh." Damon considered. "I see. And if he phoned from inside it had to go through the switchboard—"

"I doubt that. He wouldn't have done that. He'd have phoned from somewhere else. If you think it's worth the effort we'll just have to start at the top and work down."

"No effort at all," Damon said sarcastically. He walked back to the table, sat down, and aimed his gaze at a tired-looking neatly dressed man who was prematurely bald:

"Mr. Warren, I'm afraid we're not through. I want to ask some questions about your tenants. How many have you?"

"Ninety-three," the manager replied without hesitation.

"How many on the twelfth floor? That's the top, isn't it?"

"Yes. Eight."

"What are their names and who are they?"

"Well, starting at the south end, Mr. and Mrs. Raymond Bellows. Mr. Bellows has a real estate office...."

A plain-clothesman sat at the end of the table with a notebook and at the end of another hour had a voluminous record of the occupants of the top five floors of the Bolton Apartments, but there did not appear to be among them any likely candidate for the role they were trying to cast, though three or four had been reserved for further investigation. Like all searches for a nugget in a pile of what may be nothing but sand, it was a dreary and tiresome task, and most of those present were bored and half asleep when Tecumseh Fox suddenly interjected, "Ha!"

"Ha what?" Damon demanded sourly.

"That name. Mrs. Piscus."

"What about it?"

"Piscus is Latin for fish."

"The hell it is." Damon turned back to the manager. "What's she like?"

Mr. Warren gave details. Mrs. Harriet Piscus had rented 7D, which was two small rooms with bath, in January, 1939. She lived somewhere out of town, the manager didn't know where, and used the apartment only during her trips to New York, which were frequent—she made an appearance on an average of twice a week. None of the staff knew anything of her family or history. She never brought guests to her apartment and none ever called. She was prompt with the rent, which she paid in cash, generous with tips, and extremely uncommunicative. She was large of frame, shy in manner, and old-fashioned in dress, and her voice was a sort of quavery falsetto. As to her face, it was hard to say, because she always wore a thick veil. Like a mourning veil. It was the romantic assumption among the staff that the tenant of 7D came there to be alone with sorrow.

When had she last been there?

That called for discussion, but finally a doorman, a hallman and an elevator man agreed on the preceding Friday. Fox muttered something to Damon, and after the inspector muttered back he turned to the manager:

"We'll go up there and take a look at 7D."

"Now?"

"Now."

Warren protested, was told that a search warrant could not be procured until morning and requested not to enforce the delay, and reluctantly consented. Room Nine was left to its tobacco smoke and stale air, and they all emerged into the night, breathed, and filled three police cars. The trip to the Seventies took less than ten minutes through the deserted streets. The staff was told to wait downstairs, and only the manager accompanied Damon, Fox and two detectives up to 7D.

The pool contained no fish. Since the apartment was rented furnished, there was furniture there, but that was all. The closets and cupboards were bare; there was even no toothbrush in the bathroom cabinet. After a hurried

but thorough inspection, during which doorknobs and
drawer pulls were touched only with gloves, the manager
stated that every article in the place was the property of
his employers.

Damon scowled at a detective: "Get busy. Fox and I'll
go down and ask foolish questions."

In the manager's office at the rear of the lobby the staff
was collected and tackled again, but nothing new was
learned of Mrs. Harriet Piscus. None of them had ever
seen her without the veil. None had ever suspected she
was a man, though now they admitted it was quite
possible—she walked like one and she had big feet. She
always arrived in a taxi....She never phoned from her
apartment or was called there....No mail ever came for
her and no packages were delivered....

Shortly after the assemblage was dismissed the detectives came downstairs and reported: "Not a damn thing.
Not a scrap. Not a single print on anything anywhere."

Fox grunted, "Gone for the duration."

"And now," Damon said bitterly, "the police will investigate. We'll find taxi drivers who picked her up in front of
the Public Library. Fine. After losing a night's sleep what
do I know that I didn't know before? That Piscus means
fish."

"Oh, I know more than that," Fox declared. "Lots
more. For example, that fish have gills. As in Ted Gill. Or
that Dolphie or Dolphin is a common diminutive for men
named Adolph, and a dolphin is a fish—"

"Nuts," Damon said, and stamped out.

# 15

FOR THREE days a hundred detectives plodded or darted
around, as their various natures impelled them, in a
dogged and desperate search for the spoor of Mr. Fish—or

rather, of Mrs. Harriet Piscus. They found traces but no trail. A dozen taxi drivers were unearthed who had picked up a person in female clothing, wearing a mourning veil, and driven her to the Bolton Apartments. The pickups had all been in the midtown section, mostly, it appeared, near subway kiosks. All efforts to back-trail had failed. Another trace was discovered at the address on 51st Street where Fox had gone Monday night expecting to occupy a bed and had found that Perry Dunham's apartment had been visited by a hurricane. On that afternoon, Monday, the elevator had had a passenger meeting the specifications; the operator remembered it because the passenger had alighted at the third floor, where a small salon had a showing of racing prints, and he had thought it odd that a woman in mourning should be out after pictures of race horses. To walk upstairs from the third to the sixth would have been simple, though there would still have remained the detail of getting into the Dunham apartment.

The third and last race, though a dead end like the others, was the most significant of all—at least to Tecumseh Fox, when Inspector Damon told him about it. With stubborn and inexhaustible patience a squad had been assigned to recheck recent sales of potassium cyanide, and had learned that on Monday morning a clerk at Dickson's, the wholesale chemists on Second Avenue, had sold 500 cubic centimeters of oil of mirbane to a big woman with a squeaky voice wearing a mourning veil.

Damon was half frantic. "It was her," he declared with gloomy conviction. "Don't tell me it wasn't!"

"Him," Fox corrected.

"Okay, him! And he's got it and he's a murderer and he's going to use it! You know what oil of mirbane is, it's nitrobenzene, and it's so deadly that if you just drop a spoonful on your skin..."

Fox pretended to listen to a recital of the properties of nitrobenzene and the apprehensions of the inspector regarding the use Fish-Piscus intended to make of that particular bottle of it. He did not share the apprehensions, for he judged that it had taken all of 500 cubic centimeters to make the splash that had so narrowly missed him when he pushed Diego Zorilla's door open Monday afternoon. But still he restrained the impulse to relieve the inspector's mind, knowing that no subtlety or brutality of police technique could loosen Diego's tongue.

However, it was beginning to look as if Diego was the only hope. Fox had handed Mr. Fish over to the police because it was precisely the sort of thing their methods and equipment can handle vastly better than any private cleverness; and they had failed, which was astonishing. If Fish-Piscus was a man and a murderer, he was either the luckiest or the shrewdest one on the long list Fox had known.

And Inspector Damon, in something approaching a panic at the news that Piscus, presumably in his proper and unknown guise, was freshly armed with a bottle of nitrobenzene, had lost his head. The preceding evening, Friday, he had gone to Garda Tusar and exposed his hand by making a direct attack. Garda had smilingly told him that she got phone calls from many people, but not, as far as she could remember, from anyone named Fish; Frida was always getting names wrong; surely she was not legally or morally obliged to justify her practice of giving her maid an afternoon off now and then; she had never seen or heard of Mrs. Harriet Piscus. She had few contacts with the other tenants.

To Fox, Damon confessed that the frontal assault had been a blunder. In spite of the shadowing of Garda which had been ordered, Fish-Piscus could be, and certainly would be, warned. The vigil being maintained for her-him, inside and outside of the Bolton Apartments, might as well be abandoned. Also useless now were the tailings of Beck, Pomfret, Zorilla, Gill and Koch, in hopeful expectation of a lead to some side-street furnished room and a metamorphosis there into Mrs. Harriet Piscus.

Damon's confession went further, if not to defeat, at least to stalemate. During the three days' intensive and relentless hunt for Fish-Piscus, other angles had not been neglected. They had gone the limit with Koch about the vase, Hebe Heath about the violin and the whisky bottle, Dora about the second note Jan Tusar had or hadn't left, with everyone about everything, including Mrs. Pomfret about the private life of her son. The press was getting sarcastic and the police commissioner outspoken; and Irene Dunham Pomfret had an appointment to see the mayor at ten o'clock in the morning, together with the district attorney.

And Damon was lighting cigarettes and crushing them out not half smoked. That was more significant than any verbal confession whatever. Fox had seen him do that only once before, during the Hatcher case four years ago, and that case was still unsolved.

So, Fox decided as he drove uptown, the only hope was Diego. Either another try at Diego or go on marking time as he had done for the past three days, waiting for the police to flush Fish-Piscus, and he had had enough of that.

But the try at Diego had to be postponed. At the address on 54th Street Fox mounted the two flights of stairs, found that the door had been equipped with a new lock, rang the bell half a dozen times, and got no response. He sat on the top step for an hour, gave it up, returned to his car, drove home, and went to bed. In the morning, Saturday, he arose at six, was headed for the city before seven, and exactly at eight o'clock put his thumb on the bell push at Diego's flat. He could hear the sound of the bell within, and in a moment a gruff call:

"Who is it?"

"Fox."

A long pause, then: "What do you want?"

"I want to talk with you and I'm going to."

Another pause, footsteps, and the door opened.

Diego was in pajamas. He had been got out of bed and he assuredly did not reciprocate his visitor's desire for a talk, but politeness was in his bones, and he opened the door wide for Fox to enter, closed it, and indicated a chair.

"This disorder," he rumbled apologetically. "I came home late. Drunk. It's chilly in here." He went to close a window and came back and sat down. "I've been rude to you on the phone. I'm sorry, but I'll have to go on being rude."

"I don't mind." Fox grinned at him. "I'm hoping to talk

you out of it. I know who killed Jan Tusar and Perry
Dunham."

Diego, bleary-eyed, hunched in his chair, blinked. He
straightened up and blinked again. "The devil you do," he
said quietly.

"Yup. I do. But I can't prove it."

"You don't have to prove it to me." Obviously Diego did
not mean to be stampeded; he intended to remain
imperturable and noncommittal; but involuntarily he pronounced a name. "Koch," he said, barely audible, and was
immediately irritated that the sound had escaped him. He
clamped his jaw and glared.

Fox shook his head. "I'm not saying. For the present.
But I assure you I know. Also I assure you that if you keep
on being chivalrous you'll only make it worse."

Diego made a harsh noise. "Chivalrous?"

"Well, whatever you want to call it. Miss Tusar didn't
steal that vase, even if she told you she did. Nor did she
try to kill you with that booby trap. But there's not a
chance in the world of keeping her out of this. I'm being
frank with you, Diego. The police haven't caught up with
me, partly because I haven't been frank with them—"

"You can be. Go ahead. Did I ask—"

"No. You were and are the Spanish cavalier. I'm not
sneering at you, I'm not even reminding you that the lady
doesn't deserve it, and anyway, you know as well as I do.
I'm just telling you that it's useless, and it will go a lot
easier, even for her, if you tell me about it now and let me
handle it. Not to mention the danger of your being
charged as an accessory—though I suppose that wouldn't
weigh with you. A more important danger is that she will
be charged as an accessory if it isn't handled right. Do you
want that?"

Diego growled.

Fox leaned forward at him. "Use your head, Diego.
Damn it, look at it straight. How did you happen to get
hold of the vase? Did she give it to you for safekeep-
ing?"

Diego said quietly, "I told you I'd have to go on being
rude."

"And I tell you I know the murderer. And you're shielding him."

"No."

"But you are!"

"No. I don't shield a murderer. I stole that vase from Pomfret and you saw it in my closet and someone came here and took it. That's all." Diego spread his palms up, a gesture he had rarely used since the accident to his fingers. "Let me alone. Won't you? Go ahead and tell the police. I won't mind that, but you—a good friend like you—it's very difficult and painful—"

"You'd better not tell them you set that nitrobenzene trap for me. They've found out who bought it."

"Thank you. That would have been foolish anyway."

"And that's all? You're not curious about who bought it? Who tried to kill you?"

"I'm not curious about anything. Anything in the world."

Fox looked at him. He had come with the intention of spending hours, all day if necessary, in an effort to get Diego to talk, but that stony face with the bloodshot eyes told him that it would be a day wasted.

"Okay," he said, and picked up his hat. "Before I go there's something else. About a year ago somebody broke one of Pomfret's vases. A Ming five-color. This has nothing to do with the one you—uh—stole. This one was broken. Do you know anything about it?"

Diego squinted at him. "Know anything? I didn't break it, if that's what you mean."

"Do you know who did?"

"No."

"Had you heard about it?"

Diego nodded. "I was there when it happened."

"When was that?"

"As you said, about a year ago. More than a year. Mrs. Pomfret had a musical in honor of a pianist named Glissinger, and there was a mob, as usual."

"Who discovered that the vase was broken?"

"I don't know. I had left. I didn't hear about it until a week later. Pomfret was still inconsolable. He wasn't going to buy any more pottery."

"Was it known who had broken it?"

"I don't remember, I wasn't especially interested, but I think not. If it was, I've forgotten or I wasn't told."

"Do you know where the vase had been kept? Which room?"

"No." Diego was scowling. "If this is some kind of a roundabout—"

"It's plenty roundabout, no question of that." Fox stood up. "Much obliged. Sorry I got you out of bed. I'll let you know if and when the cops are coming. So long."

Down on the street, he found a phone and made several calls, returned to his car and headed downtown.

Five hours later, at two in the afternoon, he was climbing the stoop to the vestibule at the address in the East Sixties where Dora Mowbray lived. It was beginning to look as if his quest for information regarding the broken vase was going to prove as barren as had all other lines of investigation both by him and by the police. Adolph Koch had been able to furnish one item for the record: that the Ming five-color, one of the finest in existence, had been kept on a low cabinet near a corner of the yellow room, but that was all, though he had been present at the musical. Hebe Heath, in a blue tea gown on a divan in their suite at the Churchill, had furnished nothing at all except a look at the scenery, since she had been in Hollywood at the time. Felix Beck had contributed a suspicion that Garda Tusar had broken the vase, because he had seen her handling it, but he admitted that it was merely a suspicion. At the Pomfrets, the master and mistress had both gone out, and neither the butler nor the secretary could add anything to the meager facts Fox already possessed. Wells did indeed drop a dark hint about Mrs. Briscoe, but Fox let it out the other ear.

If Mrs. Briscoe or any other outsider had broken that vase, he might as well give the $5,000 back to Mrs. Pomfret and go home and pitch horseshoes.

He entered the vestibule and pushed the button marked Mowbray.

# 16

DORA, SITTING on the piano bench, wrinkled her forehead, hesitated, and said, "That's funny."

Fox felt a tingling in his stomach. "What's funny about it?"

"Why—it was so long ago—and now you ask about it. Why do you ask about it now?"

"I'm curious. Something made me curious." Fox threw one knee over the other and smiled at her. "But that wasn't what you meant when you said it was funny. You mean something else. What was funny about it?"

Dora smiled back, but shook her head. "That's all I meant."

"No. It isn't. You meant there was something funny about the broken vase, not about my asking. Come on, now. Didn't you?"

"Well...yes."

"Okay. What?"

"I can't tell you."

"Why not?"

"Because that's one of the promises I made my father. You don't need to tell me it's silly, I know it is—but I did break promises I made Dad while he was alive, little ones—and since he died—I want to keep them...." She fluttered a hand.

"Did your father break the vase?"

"Oh, no!"

"Did the promise you made concern him? I mean was it to protect him from some disgraceful or dishonorable—"

"Good heavens, no!"

"Would it reflect discredit on his—"

"No, nothing like that at all." Dora gestured impatiently.

"I told you I know it's silly, but I just won't break any promises I made him, that's all."

"Well." Fox leaned back. "All right. Two men are murdered, and possibly three, but the murderer goes free because you don't want to break a silly promise you made your father."

"Murderer?" Dora goggled at him. "That's ridiculous!"

"No, it isn't."

"But it is!"

"I say it isn't, and I know a lot more about it than you do. I knew there was something phony about that broken vase before I came to ask you about it, or I wouldn't have come. I'm telling you straight, Miss Mowbray. If you keep that promise to your father you're shielding a murderer."

"But it has nothing to do with a murder!"

"It has."

"It's absurd!"

"No." Fox leaned forward at her. "Now look. Use a little common sense. Tell me about it. If it's not what I think it may be, I forget it. If it's what I suspect, you wouldn't want me to forget it. Would you?"

"No." Dora admitted reluctantly. "Not if..."

"Certainly not. Here's what I already know. On a December afternoon sixty or seventy people were guests at a musical at Mrs. Pomfret's. In the drawing room. During an intermission drinks were served in the yellow room, and after the program there were refreshments. The Ming five-color was on a low cabinet in a far corner of the yellow room. After some, perhaps all, of the guests had departed—specifically, Diego and Beck and Adolph Koch had left—it was discovered that the vase was broken. Is that correct?"

"Yes," Dora admitted. "Except that some of the guests were still there. I was."

"How many of them?"

"Just a few. Ten or twelve."

"Do you remember who they were?"

"Well..." Dora pursed her lips. "Mrs. Briscoe. Glissinger. Barbinini. And Elaine Hart, I know she was, because she was at the other end of the room with Perry when he found the vase—"

"Perry Dunham? Was it he who made the discovery?"

"Yes. The rest of us were around the fireplace when a loud whistle came from Perry across the room and he called to Mr. Pomfret to come. Then Mr. Pomfret yelled for his wife, and we all went to see what it was, and there was the vase in a dozen pieces on the floor."

"And?"

"That's all. Mr. Pomfret looked as if he was going to cry, and he couldn't speak, so Mrs. Pomfret asked us if we knew anything about it, and we said we didn't and cleared out."

"But what was funny about that?" Fox was frowning. "What was it that you regarded as funny?"

"The funny thing didn't happen there."

"Where did it happen?"

"At home. Afterwards. Dad had left before the program was over to keep an appointment, and later, when he came home to dinner, before I mentioned what had happened, he said he supposed Pomfret had sent for the police about the vase. I asked how he knew about it, and he said that on his way out he had meant to stop in the yellow room for a drink, by the door from the reception hall, but as he was about to enter he saw the reflection of Pomfret in that big mirror at the end. He stopped at the expression on Pomfret's face, and saw that he had in his hand a piece of the Ming vase, and he didn't want to be delayed by the rumpus he knew Pomfret would make, so he went on out."

"Pomfret didn't see him."

"Apparently not."

Fox had a gleam in his eye. "So the broken vase was discovered twice, by different people."

Dora nodded. "It looked that way. I told Dad he must have been mistaken, because Pomfret had said nothing about it, and he was standing there talking with us calmly and naturally when Perry called to him, and he was certainly surprised and shocked when he saw the vase, but Dad said he was positive he had seen the piece of the vase with the yellow dragon on it in Pomfret's hand. Later he asked me to promise I wouldn't mention it to anyone, and I did. He said we had all we could do to attend to the monkey business in our own lives without butting in on other people's." Dora bit her lip. "He was a wise man—and he was kind, very kind. He never liked Mr. Pomfret."

"Did he have any theory to account for that particular monkey business?"

"I don't think so. If he had he didn't tell me."

"Did he ever mention the vase again?"

"Not that I remember. I'm sure he didn't."

"Presumably Pomfret was alone in the yellow room when your father saw him?"

"Presumably. The program was going on."

"How long was it from then until the moment Perry Dunham discovered the vase?"

"Oh…" Dora considered. "Half an hour, or maybe a little more."

"Well." Fox leaned back, frowned at the keyboard, and pulled at the tip of his ear. "I suppose it's more than I had any right to expect, but it certainly isn't much in the way of proof, especially since your father is—gone."

"You said," Dora reminded him, "that if it wasn't what you thought—"

"But it is."

She looked skeptical. "What you thought it might be?"

"Exactly. Not the details of course, but the implications. It was the first scene of a comedy which later turned into a dreadful tragedy. I know it was dreadful, because I saw Jan Tusar's face when he was trying to get music out of that violin that night."

A shiver ran over Dora. "I forget that. When I can."

"I don't," Fox said grimly. Abruptly he arose. "For the present you'll have to take my word for it that you won't regret breaking the promise you made your father. If you made any others, keep them. It's a good idea. But I'll probably have to ask you to repeat it, just as you told it to me, in the presence of others. If I do, it will be under circumstances which will convince you that it's necessary. In the meantime, for God's sake don't mention it to anybody. Three murders and another attempt at one are enough."

Dora stared at him. "Three?"

Fox nodded. "Your father. I'm beginning to think that the only thing wrong with your suspicions was that they lighted on the wrong man."

# 17

AT TWO o'clock Sunday afternoon Irene Dunham Pomfret sat again in her library, at the head of the large table where boards of orchestras and hospitals and societies had so often met. Her appearance made it questionable whether this meeting would be handled with her accustomed authority and dexterity, or indeed whether she would be able to handle it at all. Two weeks ago she had been as handsome and vital, as competently and merrily alive, as any woman with a son in his twenties could possibly ask for; now she was not even a respectable ruin. There was no muscle left in her, and no tone. Her shoulders sagged, all of her sagged, and her half-dead eyes encircled by swollen red rims suggested that no remedy would serve but the final closing.

The others at the table were disposed as they had been on two previous occasions, with one notable difference, that Tecumseh Fox was in the chair formerly occupied by Perry Dunham. At Fox's left, between him and Mrs. Pomfret, was Wells, the secretary. At his right were Henry Pomfret, Hebe Heath, and Felix Beck. Across the table were Koch, Ted Gill, Dora, Diego, and Garda Tusar.

Mrs. Pomfret looked dully around. "I want," she said, in a tone that no board or committee had ever heard, "to tell you exactly why you're here. Mr. Fox told me yesterday that the police had demanded that he turn the violin over to them, as evidence. They seem to be unable to get

any other evidence of anything whatever, so they want
that. I told him to let them have it. He objected." She
gestured flabbily at a violin case on the table in front of
Fox. Her lip trembled, she stiffened it with an obvious
effort for a moment, and then gave up. She muttered,
barely audibly, "He will tell you why."

Eyes left her face and went in visible relief to that of
Fox, a less distressing sight.

Fox glanced around. "Maybe it was an excess of cau-
tion," he conceded. He opened the case and removed the
violin and placed it gently on the table. "But I felt
responsible to you folks for this thing and I wanted to clear
myself of that responsibility. As I told the police, I held it
only as an agent. I am hereby returning it to its collective
owners. You may either surrender it to the police volun-
tarily, or compel them to resort to legal process."

Felix Beck blurted, "May I look at it?"

"Certainly." Fox passed the violin along to him, in front
of Pomfret and Hebe. Beck took it and inspected it, ran
the tips of his fingers over the curve of its belly, and
suddenly twanged the E string. The thin plaintive sound
vibrated against overwrought nerves on both sides of the
table; Dora shivered and shrank; Diego growled; Mrs.
Pomfret pressed her handkerchief to her lips; Garda Tusar
snapped peevishly, "Don't do that!"

"Excuse me," Beck said, and put the violin down.

Adolph Koch, regarding Fox, cleared his throat. "If the
police want it as evidence in a murder, they can take it,
can't they?"

"Not necessarily, Mr. Koch, if we want to hang onto it.
It's valuable and it's fragile, and it's ours. We could fight a
requisition."

Koch shrugged. "It seems to me you might have done
better than collecting us here like this. Especially it's an
imposition on Mrs. Pomfret, under the circumstances.
Couldn't you merely have phoned Miss Heath and Miss
Mowbray and me?"

"I could, of course." Fox returned his gaze unsmilingly.
"But there are complications. I'll have to tell you something else before you can make an intelligent decision

about the violin. I'll have to tell you who killed Jan Tusar and Perry Dunham."

"Then," Koch observed sarcastically, "you might have waited until you were prepared to do that."

"I did. I'm prepared now."

There were startled movements, gasps, exclamations, and ten pairs of eyes stared at him. Hebe Heath clutched Felix Beck's sleeve and he jerked away. Mrs. Pomfret came up straight and was rigid.

"It's like this," Fox said conversationally. "I had a—well, call it a strong suspicion—of the identity of the murderer five days ago. Tuesday night. I learned something yesterday afternoon that made me certain of it. But I had no proof and I still haven't. It looks as if there's none to be had. So, as I say, in order that you folks may decide intelligently about the violin, I'll just tell you what I know. Of course one of you knows it already."

"One of us," Diego muttered in low-voiced ferocity.

Mrs. Pomfret was staring at Fox with her red-rimmed eyes.

"One of us?" Dora gasped.

Koch folded his arms. "This," he said, "is an amazing performance. The performance of a mountebank—"

"I don't think so," Fox protested mildly. "It seems to me the only sensible thing to do. After all, this man whom you all shake hands with is a murderer, he is ruthless and shrewd and dangerous, and even if it can't be proved to a jury I think you folks should know about it. Particularly I think Miss Tusar should know about it. In a way she has been deceived more completely and heartlessly than anyone else. If anyone had a reason to expect a square deal from him, she had, but one of his victims was her brother, and she loved her brother. Didn't you, Miss Tusar? Didn't you love your brother Jan?"

"Yes, I did," Garda snapped. "And if you can tell me—"

"I'm going to. He tricked your brother into committing suicide. When the trick was disclosed, he was afraid you might suspect him, and he sent you that note signed with a swastika. It wasn't a Nazi who sent that note."

"How do you know it wasn't?"

"Because the swastika was wrong. It was counter-clockwise instead of clockwise."

Garda's lip curled. "It was a swastika. Did you perhaps get that idea also from my maid?"

"No. All I got from your maid was news of Mr. Fish . Which brings me to the point. Mr. Fish killed your brother."

"That's a lie—"

Swift unconsidered impulse carried her that far, then she cut it off. But not in panic; her chin went up and her eyes blazed across at Fox.

"I thought," Fox said quietly, "that you denied that you knew Mr. Fish."

"I did deny it! I do deny it! I meant only—all you say is a lie!"

Diego blurted, "Who the devil is Mr. Fish? You said one of us."

"So I did." Fox glanced around. "I suppose the story of Mr. Fish is as good a place to start as any. He is a friend of Miss Tusar's who frequently visits her apartment. Or did. Only when he arrives he is no longer Mr. Fish, but has become Mrs. Harriet Piscus—please, Miss Tusar! That won't do any good. If you start a row I'll put you out and go on with it anyway. If I libel you, you can get me for it."

"We all should get you," Koch declared with emphasis. "You said one of us. Now this Fish who becomes a Mrs. Piscus—I repeat, this is an amazing performance."

"Let him go on," Mrs. Pomfret said with authority in her tone again. "Go on, Mr. Fox."

"Well," Fox resumed, "I might as well clear up this apparent contradiction. It is only apparent. Mr. Fish is one of you. He has been excessively careful to cover his tracks in visiting Miss Tusar. He phones her in advance, probably from a public booth, so that she may dismiss her maid and be alone. He goes somewhere, probably to a furnished room, though the police haven't been able to find it, emerges as a woman with a mourning veil, takes a subway, leaves it and takes a taxi to the Bolton Apartments, where, under the name of Mrs. Harriet Piscus, he rented a suite in January, 1939. He gets off the elevator at the seventh

floor, and walks up two flights to Miss Tusar's apartment.
It sounds like a lot of trouble, but it looks as if it's going to
save him from being convicted of murder. Though of
course that wasn't why he planned all that tortuosity, since
he had no intention then of murdering anyone; he planned
it to keep his visits to Miss Tusar secret."

A noise came from Diego Zorilla's throat.

Fox looked at him. "I'm sorry, Diego. You can leave if
you want to, but that's all you can do....To go on with
Mr. Fish. He loves beautiful things and is a passionate
connoisseur of pottery. He also loves Miss Tusar. He got
hold of a Wan Li black rectangular vase, from where it
belonged in this house, and took it to Miss Tusar's apartment and left it there. He wanted those two there together when he was there. He—"

"Liar!"Garda spat at him.

"No," Fox declared, "I'm not a liar, but I admit the next
few details are conjectural. It happened, though perhaps
not exactly this way. Miss Tusar kept the vase concealed
except when Mr. Fish was there, for fear some chance
caller might recognize it as the one that had been stolen
from Mr. Pomfret, but through carelessness it was in view
one day when Diego called. Diego concluded that Miss
Tusar had stolen it. Even before that he had probably
concluded that she was supporting herself luxuriously by a
series of thefts, for he needed to satisfy his mind somehow
regarding the source of her income, and distasteful as that
conclusion was, it was less so than the possible alternatives—"

"Damn you!" Diego got up. "Come with me, damn
you!"

"I can't, Diego. Not now. You could have avoided this,
old man....So Diego took the vase. Openly, of course, in
front of Miss Tusar, since he couldn't be a sneak. His
intention was to return it somehow to Pomfret, but he
postponed it until too late. Garda had to tell Mr. Fish what
had happened to the vase, and that put him in a panic, for
by now he had other and more vital secrets even than his
friendship with Miss Tusar. Two of them. Two murders he
had committed. He didn't even trust Miss Tusar any more,
not completely; what if she had told Diego how she had

got the vase? He broke into Diego's flat and got the vase,
and set a trap there to kill him which failed only because
I happened to arrive on the scene before Diego did. Mr.
Fish now wished to return the vase to Pomfret, and he did
so, deviously, by mailing it to Koch, knowing that Koch
would recognize it and take it to Pomfret. That, last
Monday, was a busy day for Mr. Fish. That same afternoon
he went to Perry Dunham's flat and went through it like a
cyclone. I don't know what he was looking for, but my
guess is that it was the second note that Jan Tusar left on
his dressing table before he shot himself. Miss Mowbray
thought she saw two notes there, but Perry Dunham claimed
there was only one. A natural inference was that Dunham
took one of them and concealed it, presumably on his
person, and if I could make that inference, as I did,
certainly Mr. Fish could. Besides, for him it was probably
no longer an inference. Undoubtedly Dunham had told
him he had it, and may even have shown it to him.
Dunham was a rash and silly young man. He knew he was
dealing with a cornered rat, and a cornered rat is a
dangerous animal, yet after confronting Mr. Fish with the
information in that note—not that he knew him as Mr.
Fish—"

"Neither do we," Henry Pomfret put in. "If we know
him at all. Of course you're welcome to the suspense...if
that's part of the stunt...."

Fox smiled at him, a thin tight smile. "Why?" he
inquired smoothly. "Is it getting a little too tough for you?"

Pomfret tried an answering smile, and his was a shade
crooked. "Tough?"

Fox nodded. "The suspense, I mean. Naturally you're
curious—for instance, about what gave me my strong
suspicion Tuesday night. I'll relieve you on that. Four
things—none very convincing by itself, but in combination
quite an argument. First, a pomfret is a fish, a spiny-
finned sooty-black fish; and piscus means fish. Second, in
choosing an alias many people are irresistibly tempted to
pick one with their own initials; and there was Harriet
Piscus and Henry Pomfret. Third, the Wan Li black
rectangular vase had somehow got to Miss Tusar's apart-

ment; and what if it hadn't been stolen at all? Fourth and by far the best, Mr. Fish had taken incredibly elaborate precautions to keep the secret of his friendship with Miss Tusar, so it must have meant crushing disaster to him to have it disclosed. That pointed, I thought, in only one direction. I was correct, wasn't I, Mrs. Pomfret? Wasn't it wise of your husband to do his utmost to keep you from learning that Miss Tusar was his mistress?"

No one stirred; no one spoke; and Mrs. Pomfret, erect again with her fixed gaze shooting past Fox at the figure on his right, was a frozen image. Pomfret was sneering at Fox, sneering indignantly and successfully at the preposterous calumny; but, feeling that other gaze, feeling it bore through him and into him, he was inexorably impelled to abandon Fox and his sneer, and meet it. He did it well; he accepted the challenge and struck at it as he could.

"No, Irene," he said huskily but not weakly. "No. I assure you. No!"

With the last "No" there was movement, but not by him. The mounting fury of Garda Tusar, too high now for words, resorted to sudden and impetuous action, and was like lightning. Her darting hand seized the neck of the violin, on the table between her and Beck, and before either Beck or Diego could move to stop her, the fragile and priceless instrument went hurtling through the air. Presumably she aimed it at Fox, but it flew high over his head, crashed against the sharp corner of a steel cabinet, and fell to the floor. Beck bounded out of his chair after it, but Fox was there first and got it.

"Great God above," Diego said. He gripped Garda's arm and pulled her down into her chair.

Fox held the violin in his hands. The beautiful belly was splintered into fragments, so that he could look inside, at the inside of the back; and that, oddly enough at that tense moment, was what he was doing. He did so for some seconds, disregarding Beck clutching at his sleeve, until Adolph Koch exclaimed:

"Damn it, are you waiting for a cue?"

Fox, ignoring him, sat down, placed the violin on the

table before him and folded his arms on it, and looked at Henry Pomfret.

"This," he said, "changes the situation entirely. I admitted that I had no proof. If Miss Tusar had sat tight I doubt if there would ever have been any. My idea was that by convincing her that you had killed her brother I could get the proof from her—enough to serve. But she has given it to me another way."

He tapped the shattered belly of the violin. "It's here. Inside here."

# 18

POMFRET SHOWED his teeth. White was on his cheeks.

His wife extended a hand and said harshly, "Let me see it."

Fox shook his head. "I'm going on a little," he said grimly. "I'm going to have the satisfaction of cleaning it up in front of him." He twisted in his seat to face Pomfret, but kept one arm across the violin. "I said a while ago that I learned something yesterday afternoon that made me sure it was you. What I learned was what I already suspected, that you broke your Ming five-color vase yourself. You did it purposely—"

"No," a voice declared. It was Adolph Koch. "I don't believe that. If you have proof that he's a murderer, you have, but he never broke that Ming deliberately. He simply couldn't."

"He did." Fox didn't look away from Pomfret. "You broke it because you had to have a good and convincing excuse to stop collecting pottery. Your wife knew too much about pottery—not as much as you, I suppose, but too much. You wanted to start collecting coins. Because you could safely pretend that you had paid a couple of thousand for a Fatimid dinar, whereas it had cost only three or four hundred. And your wife furnished the money for your coin collecting, as she had for your pottery. In that way you could clear—I don't know—say twenty thousand a year, anyway enough to serve your purpose. So you broke the Ming."

"That's a lie." Pomfret wet his lips. He was steadily meeting Fox's gaze, which must have been easier, at least, than meeting his wife's. "It's a damned lie." He showed his teeth. "By God, you'll pay for this! That transparent trick—proof—" He pointed at the violin, his finger nearly touching it. "Pretending there's proof—when there can't be—"

"I'll come to that." Fox fastened to his eyes. "First a few other things. You broke the Ming. You were seen standing in the yellow room with a piece of it in your hand more than half an hour before Perry Dunham discovered it."

"Who saw me?"

"Lawrence Mowbray."

"He is dead."

"Yes, he's dead. I suppose the vase episode made him suspicious. He may even have been clever enough to have guessed at the motive. Somehow, I don't know how, he confirmed the suspicion and learned of your relations with Miss Tusar. Your wife was his dear and old friend. He warned you to give her a square deal and threatened to tell her if you didn't. You went unobserved to his office and hit him on the head and pushed him out of a window."

"You can prove that too."

"No, I can't. That's mostly conjecture, but I wanted to say it to you and let Miss Mowbray hear it—"

"Dora!" Pomfret stretched a hand across the table. "You don't believe?..."

She didn't look at him. Her lips compressed, her fingers twisted tight, she was gazing at Fox.

"That," Fox said, "was last winter. You felt safe. But in fact you're an extraordinary combination of cleverness and stupidity. It is possible for a man to conceal, and keep forever concealed, some isolated action, but any activity continued indefinitely will sooner or later be discovered. Mowbray discovered your relations with Miss Tusar, and not long ago Jan Tusar did also. I don't know just when or how; Miss Tusar will no doubt eventually fill that gap; before the day comes for you to face a judge and jury she will probably tell much more than that, to save herself from being tried as an accessory. It may even be that he saw the Wan Li vase in his sister's apartment, as Diego did later—your vase that you had taken there yourself. Anyway, he learned about it; and he didn't like you, and he was under great obligation to your wife. He confronted you with his knowledge and gave you an ultimatum: Break off your relations with his sister or he would inform your wife. You met the threat with the calculation of a devil and the cunning of a snake; a few hours before his big concert you poured varnish into his violin. You knew his character and temperament; you knew that, engulfed in despair, he might even kill himself; and he did."

"No," Henry Pomfret said. His voice was thick. "No!" Then he made an irremediable blunder. His head turned, and not toward his wife, but away from her. "Garda!" he entreated. "Garda, I didn't!"

Mrs. Pomfret stood up, and stood straight. There was a metallic ring in her voice:

"You say you have proof?"

Fox nodded at her. "In a moment." He took Pomfret again: "So once more, as with Lawrence Mowbray, you thought you were safe, only this time there were complications. The disappearance of the violin must have worried you badly, and though I cleared that up to your satisfaction, at the same time I brought you fresh dread by my discovery of the varnish. Your fear was not that the crime might be traced to you, but that you might be suspected by Miss Tusar, and you tried to prevent that by sending her that note and directing her suspicion elsewhere— Miss Tusar! Please! Diego, hold her!"

Diego did.

Fox went on. "But the fuse had been lit and could not be extinguished. With other apprehensions already gnawing at you, you must have been close to desperation when Perry Dunham told you that Jan had in fact left a second note, that it had been addressed to your wife and had revealed the secret of your relations with Garda, and that he had it in his possession. What else did he say? The same, I imagine, as Mowbray and Jan: He demanded that you break with Garda. He knew his mother was fairly happy with you, and he cared enough for her not to want to shatter her happiness, so instead of showing the note to her he gave you a chance. He didn't know, of course, that you were a murderer. You promised him you would break with Garda, and he foolishly believed you. As I say, he didn't know you were a murderer, but even so, it was stupid of him to take a drink from a whisky bottle to which you had access at any time, and which you knew was the brand he always took."

"You know damned well," Adolph Koch said resentfully, staring at Pomfret, "that I drink bourbon sometimes!"

Hebe Heath giggled hysterically.

"So with Perry gone," Fox resumed, "you were safe again. But things were piling up and your nerves began to squeak. There was the matter of the Wan Li vase. Garda had of course told you of Diego's taking it, and you were no longer as cool and cunning as you had been. You became Mrs. Harriet Piscus again long enough to buy some nitrobenzene. Your breaking into Diego's apartment to get the vase, and to set that trap for him, was worse than risky, it was idiotic; I won't demonstrate that; think it over. For one thing, it didn't work. There was also the matter of the second note left by Jan. That was vital. You got hold of a key to Perry's apartment—when Mrs. Pomfret gave me one I noticed that there was a duplicate—got upstairs by a subterfuge, as Mrs. Piscus, and made a frantic search, but didn't find the note."

Mrs. Pomfret spoke. "My son told me that there was none. That there was only one. That Dora had been mistaken. My son never lied to me."

"He did that once, Mrs. Pomfret. A fairly white lie, as lies go." Fox maintained his gaze at Pomfret. "That note must have had you worried. I know it did me. After Perry made a grab for the violin when I left him alone with it that day, I had an idea the note might be inside it. If a glance at the note's contents that evening in the dressing-room had made him want to conceal it, and not on his person, he might easily have dropped it through one of the f-holes, and been unable to retrieve it later because the violin had disappeared. I shook the violin around, and there was nothing loose inside. I even looked inside with a pencil flash, and that was when I discovered the varnish, but no note was visible. It was dumb of me not to guess what had happened. The layer of varnish was so thick that it was still sticky after being in there six or seven hours, and the note had fluttered down to the end and adhered there. So it didn't move when I shook the violin, and it couldn't be seen through the f-hole. It's still in there."

"It—it—" A spasm ran over Pomfret's face. "It—" That was all he could get out.

Fox nodded. "It's there flat against the varnish." His tone hardened. "It's Jan's vengeance, and his sister Garda disclosed it to us. It says, 'To I.D.P. Good-bye. My death like this is an ugliness you do not deserve. Another is your husband and my sister. Stop them. I owe you this. Good-bye. Jan.'"

Garda's head fell to the table and she shook with sobs.

"Give that to me," Pomfret said in a constrained and horrible voice.

Fox made the mistake of turning his head toward her, and as he did so Pomfret sprang. He hurled himself against Fox, knocked him back in his chair, and clawed at the violin. But someone else moved too, from Pomfret's other side, and came through the air at him like a big cat for prey. Pomfret missed his grab for the violin and went down, to the floor, at Fox's feet, with Hebe Heath on top of him. Then Fox was there...and Felix Beck...and Adolph Koch...

Fox bobbed up to find Wells, the secretary, hugging the violin to his breast. Wells spoke for the first time, in a trembling voice:

"That telephone is connected, sir."

"Thanks," Fox said. "Get Spring 7-3100."

## ABOUT THE AUTHOR

REX STOUT, the creator of Nero Wolfe, was born in No-blesville, Indiana, in 1886, the sixth of nine children of John and Lucetta Todhunter Stout, both Quakers. Shortly after his birth, the family moved to Wakarusa, Kansas. He was educated in a country school, but, by the age of nine, was recognized throughout the state as a prodigy in arithmetic. Mr. Stout briefly attended the University of Kansas, but left to enlist in the Navy, and spent the next two years as a warrant officer on board President Theo-dore Roosevelt's yacht. When he left the Navy in 1908, Rex Stout began to write freelance articles, worked as a sightseeing guide and as an itinerant bookkeeper. Later he devised and implemented a school banking system which was installed in four hundred cities and towns throughout the country. In 1927 Mr. Stout retired from the world of finance and, with the proceeds of his bank-ing scheme, left for Paris to write serious fiction. He wrote three novels that received favorable reviews before turning to detective fiction. His first Nero Wolfe novel, *Fer-de-Lance*, appeared in 1934. It was followed by many others, among them, *Too Many Cooks, The Silent Speaker, If Death Ever Slept, The Doorbell Rang* and *Please Pass the Guilt*, which established Nero Wolfe as a leading character on a par with Erle Stanley Gardner's famous protagonist, Perry Mason. During World War II, Rex Stout waged a personal campaign against Nazism as chairman of the War Writers' Board, master of cere-monies of the radio program "Speaking of Liberty" and as a member of several national committees. After the war, he turned his attention to mobilizing public opinion against the wartime use of thermonuclear devices, was an active leader in the Authors' guild and resumed writing his Nero Wolfe novels. Rex Stout died in 1975 at the age of eighty-eight. A month before his death, he pub-lished his seventy-second Nero Wolfe mystery, *A Family Affair*.

Share in a publishing event!
Rex Stout's Nero Wolfe returns in

# Murder in E Minor
## by Robert Goldsborough.

Here are special advance preview chapters from
MURDER IN E MINOR, which will be available
as a Bantam hardcover on April 1, 1986, at
your local bookseller.

# I

November, 1977

Nero Wolfe and I have argued for years about whether
the client who makes his first visit to us before or after
noon is more likely to provide an interesting—and lucra-
tive—case. Wolfe contends that the average person is
incapable of making a rational decision, such as hiring
him, until he or she has had a minimum of two substantial meals that day. My own feeling is that the caller
with the greater potential is the one who has spent the
night agonizing, finally realizes at dawn that Wolfe is the
answer, and does something about it fast. I'll leave it to
you to decide, based on our past experience, which of us
has it better pegged.

I'd have been more smug about the timing of Maria
Radovich's call that rainy morning if I'd thought there
was even one chance in twenty that Wolfe would see her,
let alone go back to work. It had been more than two
years since Orrie Cather committed suicide—with Wolfe's
blessing and mine. At the time, the realization that one of
his longtime standbys had murdered three people didn't
seem to unhinge Wolfe, but since then I had come to see
that the whole business had rocked him pretty good. He
would never admit it, of course, with that ego fit for his
seventh of a ton, but he was still stung that someone who
for years had sat at his table, drunk his liquor, and followed his orders could be a cool and deliberate killer.
And even though the D.A. had reinstated both our licenses
shortly after Orrie's death, Wolfe had stuck his head in
the sand and still hadn't pulled it out. I tried needling
him back to work, a tactic that had been successful in
the past, but I got stonewalled, to use a word he hates.

"Archie," he would say, looking up from his book,
"as I have told you many times, one of your most com-
mendable attributes through the years has been your
ability to badger me into working. That former asset is

now a liability. You may goad me if you wish, but it is futile. I will not take the bait. And desist using the word 'retired.' I prefer to say that I have withdrawn from practice." And with that, he would return to his book, which currently was a re-reading of *Emma* by Jane Austen.

It wasn't that we did not have opportunities. One well-fixed Larchmont widow offered twenty grand for starters if Wolfe would find out who poisoned her chauffeur, and I couldn't even get him to see her. The murder was never solved, although I leaned toward the live-in maid, who was losing out in a triangle to the gardener's daughter. Then there was the Wall Street money man—you'd know his name right off—who said Wolfe could set his own price if only we'd investigate his son's death. The police and the coroner had called it a suicide, but the father was convinced it was a narcotics-related murder. Wolfe politely but firmly turned the man down in a ten-minute conversation in the office, and the kid's death went on the books as a suicide.

I couldn't even use the money angle to stir him. On some of our last big cases, Wolfe insisted on having the payments spread over a long period, so that a series of checks—some of them biggies—rolled in every month. That, coupled with a bunch of good investments, gave him a cash flow that was easily sufficient to operate the old brownstone on West Thirty-fifth Street near the Hudson that has been home to me for more than half my life. And operating the brownstone doesn't come cheap, because Nero Wolfe has costly tastes. They include my salary as his confidential assistant, errand boy, and—until two years ago—man of action, as well as those of Theodore Horstmann, nurse to the ten thousand orchids Wolfe grows in the plant rooms up on the roof, and Fritz Brenner, on whom I would bet in a cook-off against any other chef in the universe.

I still had the standard chores, such as maintaining the orchid germination records, paying the bills, figuring the taxes, and handling Wolfe's correspondence. But I had lots of free time now, and Wolfe didn't object to a little free-lancing. I did occasional work for Del Bascomb, a first-rate local operative, and also teamed with Saul Panzer on a couple of jobs, including the Masters kidnapping case, which you may have read about. Wolfe went so far as to compliment me on that one, so at least I knew he still read about crime, although he refused to let me talk about it in his presence anymore.

Other than having put his brain in the deep freeze, Wolfe kept his routine pretty much the same as ever: Breakfast on a tray in his room; four hours a day—9 to 11 a.m. and 4 to 6 p.m.—in the plant rooms with Theodore; long conferences with Fritz on menus and food preparation; and the best meals in Manhattan. The rest of the time, he was in his oversized chair behind his desk in the office reading and drinking beer. And refusing to work.

Maria Radovich's call came at nine-ten on Tuesday morning, which meant Wolfe was up with the plants. Fritz was in the kitchen, working on one of Wolfe's favorite lunches, sweetbreads in bechamel sauce and truffles. I answered at my desk, where I was balancing the checkbook.

"Nero Wolfe's residence. Archie Goodwin speaking."

"I need to see Mr. Wolfe—today. May I make an appointment?" It was the voice of a young woman, shaky, and with an accent that seemed familiar to me.

"I'm sorry, but Mr. Wolfe isn't consulting at the present time," I said, repeating a line I had grown to hate.

"Please, it's important that I see him. I think my—"

"Look, Mr. Wolfe isn't seeing any one, honest. I can suggest some agencies if you're looking for a private investigator."

"No, I want Mr. Nero Wolfe. My uncle has spoken of him, and I am sure he would want to help. My uncle knew Mr. Wolfe many years ago in Montenegro; and—"

"Where?" I barked it out.

"In Montenegro. They grew up there together. And now I am frightened about my uncle . . ."

Ever since it became widely known that Wolfe had retired—make that withdrawn from practice—would-be clients had cooked up some dandy stories to try to get him working again. I was on their side, but I knew Wolfe well enough to realize that almost nothing would bring him back to life. This was the first time, though, that anyone had been ingenious enough to come up with a Montenegro angle, and I admire ingenuity.

"I'm sorry to hear that you're scared," I said, "but Mr. Wolfe is pretty hard-hearted. I've got a reputation as a softie, though. How soon can your uncle be here? I'm Mr. Wolfe's confidential assistant, and I'll be glad to see him, Miss . . ."

"Radovich, Maria Radovich. Yes, I recognized your name. My uncle doesn't know I am calling. He would be angry. But I will come right away, if it's all right."

I assured her it was indeed all right and hung up, staring at the open checkbook. It was a long-shot, no question, but if I had anything to lose by talking to her, I couldn't see it. And just maybe, the Montenegro bit was for real. Montenegro, in case you don't know, is a small piece of Yugoslavia, and it's where Wolfe comes from. He still has relatives there; I send checks to three of them every month. But as for old friends, I doubted any were still alive. His closest friend ever, Marko Vukcic, had been murdered years ago, and the upshot was that Wolfe and I went tramping off to the Montenegrin mountains to avenge his death. And although Wolfe was anything but gabby about his past, I figured I knew just about enough to eliminate the possibility of a close comrade popping up. But there's no law against hoping.

I got a good, leisurely look at her through the one-way panel in the front door as she stood in the drizzle ringing our bell. Dark-haired, dark-eyed, and slender, she had a touch of Mia Farrow in her face. And like Farrow in several of her roles, she seemed frightened and unsure. But looking through the glass, I was convinced that with Maria Radovich, it was no act.

She jumped when I opened the door. "Oh! Mr. Goodwin?"

"The selfsame," I answered with a slight bow and an earnest smile. "And you are Maria Radovich, I presume? Please come in out of the twenty-percent chance of showers."

I hung her trenchcoat on the hall rack and motioned toward the office. Walking behind her, I could see that her figure, set off by a skirt of fashionable length, was a bit fuller than I remembered Mia Farrow's to be, and that was okay with me.

"Mr. Wolfe doesn't come down to the office for another hour and ten minutes," I said, motioning to the yellow chair nearest my desk. "Which is fine, because he wouldn't see you anyway. At least not right now. He thinks he's retired from the detective business. But I'm not." I flipped open my notebook and swiveled to face her.

"I'm sure if Mr. Wolfe knew about my uncle's trouble, he would want to do something right away," she said, twisting a scarf in her lap and leaning forward tensely.

"You don't know him, Miss Radovich. He can be immovable, irascible, and exasperating when he wants to, which is most of the time. I'm afraid you're stuck with me, at least for now. Maybe we can get Mr. Wolfe interested, later, but to do that, I've got to know everything. Like for starters, who is your uncle and why are you worried about him?"

"He is my great-uncle, really," she answered, still using only the front quarter of the chair cushion. "And he is very well-known. Milan Stevens. I am sure you have heard of him—he is music director, some people say conductor, of the New York Symphony."

Not wanting to look stupid or disappoint her, or both, I nodded. I've been to the symphony four or five times, always with Lily Rowan, and it was always her idea. Milan Stevens may have been the conductor one or more of those times, but I wouldn't take an oath on it. The name was only vaguely familiar.

"Mr. Goodwin, for the last two weeks, my uncle has been getting letters in the mail—awful, vile letters. I think someone may want to kill him, but he just throws the letters away. I am frightened. I am sure that—"

"How many letters have there been, Miss Radovich? Do you have any of them?"

She nodded and reached into the shoulder bag she had set on the floor. "Three so far, all the same." She handed the crumpled sheets over, along with their envelopes, and I spread them on my desk. Each was on six-by-nine-inch notepaper, plain white, the kind from an inexpensive tear-off pad. They were hand-printed, in all caps, with a black felt-tip pen. One read:

MAESTRO
QUIT THE PODIUM NOW! YOU ARE DOING
DAMAGE TO A GREAT ORCHESTRA PUT
DOWN THE BATON AND GET OUT IF YOU
DON'T LEAVE ON YOUR OWN, YOU WILL BE
REMOVED—PERMANENTLY!

In fact, all three weren't exactly alike. The wording differed, though only slightly. The "on your own" in the last sentence was missing from one note, and the first sentence didn't have an exclamation point in another. Maria had lightly penciled the numbers 1, 2, and 3 on the backs of each to indicate the order in which they were received. The envelopes were of a similar ordinary stock, each hand-printed to Milan Stevens at an address in the East Seventies. "His apartment?" I asked.

Maria nodded. "Yes, he and I have lived there since we came to this country, a little over two years ago."

"Miss Radovich, before we talk more about these notes, tell me about your uncle, and yourself. First, you said on the phone that he and Mr. Wolfe knew each other in Montenegro."

She eased back into the chair and nodded. "Yes, my uncle—his real name is Stefanovic, Milos Stefanovic. We are from Yugoslavia. I was born in Belgrade, but my uncle is a Montenegrin. That's a place on the Adriatic. But of course I don't have to tell you that—I'm sure you know all about it from Mr. Wolfe.

"My uncle's been a musician and conductor all over Europe—Italy, Austria, Germany. He was conducting in London last, before we came here. But long ago, he did some fighting in Montenegro. I know little of it, but I think he was involved in an independence movement. He doesn't like to talk about that at all, and he never mentioned Mr. Wolfe to me until one time when his picture was in the papers. It was something to do with a murder or a suicide—I think maybe your picture was there too?"

I nodded. That would have been when Orrie died. "What did your uncle say about Mr. Wolfe?"

"I gather they had lost touch over the years. But he didn't seem at all interested in getting in touch with Mr. Wolfe. At the time I said, 'How wonderful that such an old friend is right here. What a surprise! You'll call him, of course?' But Uncle Milos said no, that was part of the past. And I got the idea from the way he acted that they must have had some kind of difference. But that was so long ago!"

"If you sensed your uncle was unfriendly toward Mr. Wolfe, what made you call?"

"After he told me about knowing Mr. Wolfe back in

Montenegro, Uncle Milos kept looking at the picture in the paper and nodding his head. He said to me, 'He had the finest mind I have ever known. I wish I could say the same for his disposition.' "

I held back a smile. "But you got the impression that your uncle and Mr. Wolfe were close at one time?"

"Absolutely," Maria said. "Uncle Milos told me they had been through some great difficulty together. He even showed me this picture from an old scrapbook." She reached again into her bag and handed me a gray-toned photograph mounted on cardboard and ragged around the edges.

They certainly fit my conception of a band of guerrillas, although none looked to be out of his teens. There were nine in all, posed in front of a high stone wall, four kneeling in front and five standing behind them. Some were wearing long overcoats, others had on woolen shirts, and two wore what I think of as World War I helmets. I spotted Wolfe instantly, of course. He was second from the left in the back row, with his hands behind his back and a bandolier slung over one shoulder. His hair was darker then, and he weighed at least one hundred pounds less, but the face was remarkably similar to the one I had looked at across the dinner table last night. And his glare had the same intensity, coming at me from a faded picture, that it does in the office when he thinks I'm badgering him.

To Wolfe's right in the photo was Marko Vukcic, holding a rifle loosely at his side. "Which one's your uncle?" I asked Maria.

She leaned close enough so I could smell her perfume and pointed to one of the kneelers in front. He was dark-haired and intense like most of the others, but he appeared smaller than most of them. None of the nine, though, looked as if he were trying to win a congeniality contest. If they were as tough as they appeared, I'm glad I wasn't fighting against them.

"This picture was taken up in the mountains," Maria said. "Uncle Milos only showed it to me to point out Mr. Wolfe, but he wouldn't talk any more about the other men or what they were doing."

"Not going to a picnic," I said. "I'd like to hang onto this for a while. Now, what about you, Miss Radovich?

How does it happen you're living with a great-uncle?"

She told me about how her mother, a widow, had died when she was a child in Yugoslavia, and that Stefanovic, her mother's uncle, had legally adopted her. Divorced and without children, he was happy to have the companionship of a nine-year-old. Maria said he gave her all the love of a parent, albeit a strict one, taking her with him as he moved around Europe to increasingly better and more prestigious conducting jobs. At some time before moving to England, he had changed his name to Stevens—she couldn't remember exactly when. It was while they were living in London that he was picked as the new conductor, or music director if you prefer, of the New York Symphony. Maria, who by that time was twenty-three, made the move with him, and she was now a dancer with a small troupe in New York.

"Mr. Goodwin," she said, leaning forward and tensing again, "my uncle has worked hard all his life to get the kind of position and recognition he has today. Now somebody is trying to take it away from him." Her hand gripped my forearm.

"Why not just go to the police?" I asked with a shrug.

"I suggested that to Uncle Milos, and he became very angry. He said it would leak out to the newspapers and cause a scandal at the symphony, that the publicity would be harmful to him and the orchestra. He says these notes are from a crazy person, or maybe someone playing a prank. I was with him when he opened the first one, or I might not know about any of this. He read it and said something that means 'stupid' in Serbo-Croatian, then crumpled the note and threw it in the wastebasket. But he hardly spoke the rest of the evening.

"I waited until he left the room to get the note from the basket. It was then that I said we should call the police. He became upset and said it was probably a prankster, or maybe a season-ticket holder who didn't like the music the orchestra had been playing."

"How long until the next note?" I asked.

"I started watching the mail after that. Six days later, we got another envelope printed just like the first one. I didn't open it—I never open my uncle's mail. But again I found the crumpled note in the wastebasket next to his desk in the library. This time I didn't mention it to him, and he said nothing about it to me, but again he seemed distressed.

"The third note came yesterday, six days after the second, and again I found it in the wastebasket. Uncle Milos doesn't know that I've seen the last two notes, or that I've saved all three."

"Miss Radovich, does your uncle have any enemies you know of, anyone who would gain by his leaving the symphony?"

"The music director of a large orchestra always has his detractors." She took a deep breath. "There are always people who think it can be done better. Some are jealous, others just take pleasure in scoffing at talented people. My uncle does not discuss his work very much at home, but I do know, from him and from others, that he has opposition even within the orchestra. But notes like this, I can't believe—"

"*Someone* is writing them, Miss Radovich. I'd like to hear more about your uncle's opposition, but Mr. Wolfe will be down in just a few minutes, and it's best if you're not here when he comes in. He may get interested in your problem, but you'll have to let me be the one to try getting him interested."

For the third time, Maria dove into her bag. She fished out a wad of bills and thrust it at me. "There's five hundred dollars here," she said. "That is just for agreeing to try to find out who's writing the notes. I can pay another forty-five hundred dollars if you discover the person and get him to stop." Five grand was a long way below what Wolfe usually got as a fee, but I figured that for Maria Radovich, it was probably big bucks. I started to return the money, then I drew back and smiled.

"Fair enough," I said. "If I can get Nero Wolfe to move, we keep this. Otherwise, it goes back to you. Now we've got to get you out of here. You'll be hearing from me soon—one way or the other." I wrote her a receipt for the money, keeping a carbon, and hustled her out to the hall and on with her coat.

My watch said ten fifty-eight as she went down the steps to the street. I rushed back to the office, put the money and receipt in the safe, and arranged Wolfe's morning mail in a pile on his blotter. Included in the stack was one item the carrier hadn't delivered: a faded fifty-year-old photograph.

# 2

I just had time to get my paper in the typewriter and start on yesterday's dictation when I heard the elevator coming down from the plant rooms. "Good morning, Archie, did you sleep well?" he asked as he walked across to his desk, arranged a raceme of orchids in the vase, then settled his bulk into the only chair he likes and rang for beer.

"Yes sir," I answered, looking up. Despite his size, and we're talking about a seventh of a ton here, I've never gotten used to how efficient Wolfe is when he moves. Somehow, you keep thinking he's going to trip or do something clumsy when he goes around behind his desk, but he never does. Everything is smooth, even graceful— if you can use that word with someone so large. Then there are his clothes. Fat people get a rap for being sloppy, but not Nero Wolfe. Today, as usual, he was wearing a three-piece suit, this one a tan tweed, with a fresh yellow shirt and a brown silk tie with narrow yellow stripes. His wavy hair, still brown but with a healthy dose of gray mixed in, was carefully brushed. He'd never admit it to me or anybody else, but Nero Wolfe spent his share of time in front of the mirror every morning, and that included shaving with a straight razor, something I quit trying years ago when I got tired of the sight of my own blood.

I kept sneaking glances at Wolfe while he riffled through the stack of mail. The photograph was about halfway down, but he took his time getting there, stopping as I knew he would to peruse a seed catalog. I typed on.

"Archie!" It was a high-grade bellow, the first one he'd uncorked in months.

I looked up, feigning surprise.

"Where did this come from?" he asked, jabbing at the picture.

"What's that, sir?" I raised one eyebrow, which always gets him because he can't do it.

"You know very well. How did this get here? What envelope was it in?"

"Oh, *that*. Well, let me think . . . yes, of course, I almost forgot. It was brought by a young woman, nice-looking, too. She thought you might be interested in helping her with a problem."

Wolfe glowered, then leaned forward and studied the photograph. "They must all be dead by now . . . Two were killed by firing squads, one died in a foolhardy duel, another drowned in the Adriatic. And Marko . . ."

"They're not *all* dead," I put in. "You aren't, not legally anyway, although you've been putting on a good imitation for a couple of years. And there's at least one other living man in that picture."

Wolfe went back to the photograph, this time for more than a minute. "*Stefanovic.*" He pronounced it far differently than I would have. "I have no knowledge of his death."

"You win a case of salt-water taffy," I said. "Not only is he still breathing, but he lives right here in New York. And what's more, he's famous. Of course he's changed his name since you knew him."

Wolfe shot me another glower. His index finger was tracing circles on the arm of the chair, the only outward indication that he was furious. I knew more than he did about something and was forcing him to ask questions, which made it even worse.

"Archie, I have suffered your contumacy for longer than I care to think about." He pursed his lips. "Confound it, report!"

"Yes, sir," I said, maintaining a somber expression. Then I unloaded everything verbatim, from Maria's phone call to the money. When I got to the part about the three notes. I opened the safe and pulled them out, but he refused to give them a glance. During my whole report, he sat with his eyes closed, fingers interlaced on his center mound. He interrupted twice to ask questions. When I was through, he sat in silence, eyes still closed.

After about five minutes, I said, "Are you asleep, or just waiting for me to call in a portrait painter so he can capture your favorite pose?"

"Archie, shut up!" That made it two bellows in one day. I was trying to think up something smart to say that would bring on a third and set a record, but Fritz came in and announced lunch.

Wolfe has a rule, never broken, that business is not to be discussed during meals, and it had been an easy rule to keep for the last two years, since there wasn't any business. That day, though, my mind was on other things and I barely tasted Fritz's superb sweetbreads. Wolfe, however, consumed three helpings at his normal, unhurried pace, while holding forth on the reasons why third parties have been unsuccessful in American elections.

We finally went back to the office for coffee. During lunch, I decided I'd pushed Wolfe enough and would leave the next move to him. We sat in silence for several minutes, and I was beginning to revise my strategy when he got up and went to the bookshelf. He pulled down the big atlas, lugged it back to his desk, and opened it. He looked at a page, then turned back to the photograph, fingering it gently.

"Archie?" He drew in a bushel of air, then let it out slowly.

"Yes, sir?"

"You know Montenegro, at least superficially."

"Yes, sir."

"You also know—I have told you—that in my youth there, I was impetuous and headstrong, and that I sometimes showed a pronounced lack of judgment."

"So you have said."

"A half-century ago in Montenegro, Milos Stefanovic and I were relatively close friends, although I never shared his consuming interest in music. We fought together, along with Marko and others in the photograph, for a cause in which we strongly believed. On one occasion in Cetinje, Stefanovic saved my life. And then, for reasons that are now irrelevant, he and I parted, not without rancor. I haven't seen him since that time, and I probably haven't thought about him for twenty years, at least. I mention this by way of telling you that we are faced with an extraordinary circumstance."

"Yes, sir." Although Wolfe's upstairs horsepower is far greater than mine, I've been around long enough to know when he's rationalizing. I stifled a smile.

"I am duty-bound to see this woman." He spread his hands in what for him is a dramatic gesture of helplessness. "I have no choice. Tell her to be here at three o'clock. Also, it's been a long time since Mr. Cohen has joined us for dinner. Call and invite him for tonight. And tell him we will be serving that cognac he enjoys so much."

I was delighted, of course, that Wolfe had agreed to see Maria. But his wanting Lon Cohen to come for dinner was a bonus. Lon works for the *Gazette*, where he has an office two doors from the publisher's on the twentieth floor. He doesn't have a title I'm aware of, but I can't remember a major story in New York that he didn't know more about than ever appeared in the *Gazette*, or anyplace else, for that matter. Lon and I play in the same weekly poker game, but he only comes to dinner at Wolfe's a couple of times a year, and it's almost always when Wolfe wants information. This is all right with Lon, because he's gotten a fat file of exclusive stories from us through the years, not to mention some three-star meals.

As it turned out, Lon was available, although he wanted to know what was up. I told him he'd just have to wait, and that there was some Remisier to warm his tummy after dinner. He said for that he'd sell any state secrets he had lying around the office. And Maria could make it at three. "Does this mean Mr. Wolfe will take the case?" she asked over the phone breathlessly.

"Who knows?" I answered. "But at least he'll see you, and that alone is progress."

I went to the kitchen to tell Fritz there would be a guest for dinner. "Archie, things are happening today, I can tell. Is he going back to work?"

Fritz always fusses when Wolfe is in one of his periodic relapses. He acts like we're on the brink of bankruptcy at all times and thinks that if Wolfe isn't constantly performing feats of detection, there won't be enough money to pay his salary or, more important, the food bills. Needless to say, the last two years of inactivity by Wolfe had left Fritz with a permanently long puss, and I more than once caught him in the kitchen wringing his hands, looking heavenward, and muttering things in

French. "Archie, he needs to work," Fritz would say. "He enjoys his food more then. Work sharpens his appetite." I always replied that his appetite seemed plenty sharp to me, but he just shook his head mournfully.

This time, though, I delighted to report that prospects were improving. "Keep your carving knives crossed," I told him, "and say a prayer to Brillat-Savarin."

"I'll do more than that," he said. "Tonight, you and Mr. Wolfe and Mr. Cohen will have a dinner to remember." Whistling, he turned to his work, and I whistled a bit myself on the way back to the office.

# NERO WOLFE

He's not much to look at and he'll never win the hundred yard dash but for sheer genius at unraveling the tangled skeins of crime he has no peer. His outlandish adventures make for some of the best mystery reading in paperback. He's the hero of these superb suspense stories.

# BY REX STOUT

| | | |
|---|---|---|
| ☐ 23931 | AND BE A VILLAIN | $2.50 |
| ☐ 24985 | AND FOUR TO GO | $2.95 |
| ☐ 24730 | DEATH OF A DUDE | $2.95 |
| ☐ 24122 | A FAMILY AFFAIR | $2.95 |
| ☐ 24728 | THE FATHER HUNT | $2.95 |
| ☐ 24918 | FER-DE-LANCE | $2.95 |
| ☐ 24919 | THE RED BOX | $2.95 |
| ☐ 25127 | THREE DOORS TO DEATH | $2.95 |
| ☐ 29547 | THREE MEN OUT | $2.95 |
| ☐ 25066 | TOO MANY WOMEN | $2.95 |
| ☐ 25174 | GAMBIT | $2.95 |
| ☐ 24884 | MURDER BY THE BOOK | $2.95 |
| ☐ 24959 | THREE WITNESSES | $2.95 |
| ☐ 24438 | CHAMPAGNE FOR ONE | $2.50 |
| ☐ 24375 | IN THE BEST OF FAMILIES | $2.50 |
| ☐ 24269 | PRISONER'S BASE | $2.50 |
| ☐ 24032 | A RIGHT TO DIE | $2.50 |
| ☐ 24594 | THE SECOND CONFESSION | $2.95 |
| ☐ 24813 | THREE FOR THE CHAIR | $2.95 |
| ☐ 24498 | CURTAINS FOR THREE | $2.95 |

**Prices and availability subject to change without notice.**

Buy them at your local bookstore or use this handy coupon for ordering: